F.W. HARVEY

A WAR
ROMANCE

F.W. HARVEY

A WAR ROMANCE

The Lost Novel of F.W. Harvey

The History Press

This novel was discovered as a result of a collaborative project between Gloucestershire Archives, University of Exeter and the F.W. Harvey Society and by kind permission of Eileen Griffiths, the daughter of F.W. Harvey.

First published 2014

The History Press
The Mill, Brimscombe Port
Stroud, Gloucestershire, GL5 2QG
www.thehistorypress.co.uk

© F.W. Harvey, 2014

The right of F.W. Harvey to be identified as the Author
of this work has been asserted in accordance with the
Copyright, Designs and Patents Act 1988.

British Library Cataloguing in Publication Data.
A catalogue record for this book is available from the British
Library.

ISBN 978 0 7509 5971 1

Typesetting and origination by The History Press
Printed in Great Britain

CONTENTS

FOREWORD

Poet and composer Ivor Gurney was a patient at the City of London Mental Hospital on 20 October 1925, the day he received a visit from Helen Thomas, the widow of another poet of the First World War, Edward Thomas. She was escorted to the hospital by Gurney's steadfast friend, Marion Scott. Scott had arranged the meeting, perhaps hoping that it might provide him with some momentary relief from the bouts of intolerable mental illness that he suffered from. Gurney was lucid that day, and Helen Thomas had a 'wonderful time' speaking with him about their mutual admiration for her late husband's poems, some of which Gurney hoped soon to set to music. This clearly meant much to the widow, who asked Gurney, 'Is there anything I can do for you – anything that would give you pleasure?' Without hesitation, Gurney replied, 'Don't do it for me – do it for Harvey. Please get a publisher to publish his novel.'[1]

Though suffering from extreme mental illness and the tedium of a life in confinement, Gurney's compassionate thoughts drifted to the disappointment felt by his best friend, F.W. Harvey, for having failed to find a publisher for his war novel. Gurney would remain in the City of London Mental Hospital until his death in 1937. Harvey was still approaching publishers about the novel until that same year.[2] He then seems to have given up, and the novel was forgotten.

Despite this singular failure, Harvey had many literary successes to be proud of. He had gained national fame with his poetry written during the First World War and he had played a key role in founding the first of the British trench journals, the *5th Gloucester Gazette* – the voice of the 1/5th Battalion, Gloucestershire Regiment. The periodical's debut came on 12 April 1915 in the front lines of Ploegsteert,

Belgium. Harvey provided much of the copy that kept the paper alive in its infancy; he would eventually publish seventy-seven poems there. This led to Harvey's poetry attracting the attention of national publications: the critic and anthologist E.B. Osborn observed in *The Times Literary Supplement* that Harvey's poetry helped to make the *5th Gloucester Gazette* 'the most literary of the British trench journals'.[3]

The positive reception of Harvey's work led the well-known firm Sidgwick & Jackson to publish his first poetry collection, *A Gloucestershire Lad at Home and Abroad*, in September 1916. The volume was primarily a reprinting of his poems from the *5th Gloucester Gazette*. It saw excellent sales, going into six impressions over three years.[4] Sales were aided by Harvey's reputation as a soldier: he had earned the Distinguished Conduct Medal (DCM)[5] during a night-time trench raid in August 1915, and only a month before the collection's release he was captured by the Germans and made a prisoner during a daring solo reconnaissance mission. September 1917 saw the publication of his second collection, *Gloucestershire Friends: Poems from a German Prison Camp*. German prison camp authorities had allowed Harvey to mail poetry manuscripts home and to correspond with his de facto literary agent, Bishop George Frodsham, Canon Residentiary of Gloucester Cathedral. *Gloucestershire Friends* has the distinction of being the only collection of First World War poetry to be published while the author was a prisoner of war.

Following his release at the end of the war, Harvey returned to his beloved Gloucestershire, and in 1919 published another collection, *Ducks, and Other Verses*. Many of its poems were also written in prison camps, including his most famous, 'Ducks'. In 1920 he produced an autobiographical account of his time as a prisoner of war, titled *Comrades in Captivity*. Both saw disappointing sales, as a war-weary public had lost interest in such works. Still, these were followed by further poetry collections: *Farewell* in 1921 and *September and Other Poems* in 1925. Harvey's poetic output began to decline at this time, due to the demands of a legal career and family life. *September* would be his last major publication with Sidgwick & Jackson, as the firm began to doubt his commercial viability. Despite this, many of his poems continued to feature in popular anthologies, and do to this day. His *In Pillowell Woods* (1926) was published by a small, local publisher in Lydney, Gloucestershire, and was largely forgotten. The last volume of Harvey's poetry that he would live to see printed, simply titled *Gloucestershire*, was published by Oliver & Boyd in 1946.

Harvey died in 1957 aged 68, at which point his property, including his house of Highview at Yorkley, passed to his son, Patrick. The legacy included his personal papers, which contained the manuscript of this novel. Patrick was highly protective and kept the papers largely sequestered away from the public eye.

When Patrick died in 2007 ownership of Highview passed to F.W. Harvey's daughter, Eileen Griffiths, and her daughter, Elaine Jackson. They discovered Harvey's papers there, including the manuscript of this novel, tucked away in a chest. They appointed Roger Deeks and Teresa Davies, both leading members of the F.W. Harvey Society, as trustees of the collection to see that the papers were preserved at the Gloucestershire Archives. Through their work, and that of archives directors, the papers were brought to the attention of Professor Tim Kendall, Head of English at the University of Exeter. He secured funding to support a doctoral researcher to work at Gloucestershire Archives to catalogue, preserve and study the papers, and to complete a dissertation on F.W. Harvey's work. Appointed to this role, I was given the opportunity to be the first academic researcher to have access to a cornucopia of literary and historical treasures.

The novel was the most surprising find among the papers. It was thought that *Comrades in Captivity* was Harvey's only serious venture into prose. Yet here was a full novel, as well as dozens of short stories, essays and notes for lectures, ranging across a variety of topics and genres. From the hundreds of letters found with the papers – including the letter from Marion Scott mentioned earlier in this foreword – we can begin to piece together the history of this novel. Letters from Sidgewick & Jackson, and from Gurney, indicate that Harvey began work on it as early as 1920. Gurney's comments above indicate that the novel had been finished and rejected by publishers by 1925. In 1935 Harvey contracted a former wartime comrade, N.F. Nicholas, to act as his agent in a new attempt to find a publisher.[6] It seems that Nicholas was responsible for the creation of the surviving typescript that is presented here. In 1937 Nicholas returned the typescript, writing that no publishers were interested.[7] Harvey shelved the novel at that point and never mentioned it again in correspondence. Surely this disappointment was compounded when Harvey's great friend, Ivor Gurney, died in the asylum that same year. (A letter from Scott informing Harvey of Gurney's death was also found among these papers – it was torn in half.)[8] The novel then lay unread among Harvey's papers until their rediscovery.

Harvey's Author's Note states that the novel is fictional, but semi-autobiographical. The novel's value comes from analysis of which characters and events are based on reality, and which were purely the author's invention.

The Author's Note also states that none of the characters in the story were based on still-living people at the time of writing. This is not entirely true. The character 'Will' or 'Willie' was clearly based on Harvey himself, who was known as Will to family and friends. There is also his mother, who is a significant character in the book. Contemporary accounts of her align very closely to the character as described in the novel. Her death in the novel is an invention, as Cecilia Matilda Harvey did not die until 1942. Ivor Gurney fleetingly appears twice in the novel, though otherwise remains absent.

The most prominent character aside from Will is his brother Eric. In reality, Eric served with distinction in the Gloucestershire Regiment, earning a Military Cross and Bar,[9] but was killed in the final offensive on the Western Front in October 1918. That same month Harvey, still a prisoner of war in Germany, was preparing for movement to neutral Holland through a prisoner-exchange programme. His papers show that he received the letter informing him of Eric's death either just as he was leaving Germany or immediately after arriving in Holland.[10] In *Comrades in Captivity*, Harvey stated that 'the whole sting of [the prisoner's] position, that which makes it so intolerable, is ... his friends and brothers are "out there" killing and being killed. *He* cannot help them. He is futile ... There is no more terrible reflection for a man.'[11] This guilt was compounded in the case of his brothers (his youngest living brother, Roy, was also fighting). In this novel, Harvey does not go so far as to save Eric from his fate, but he does at least save himself from the guilt of being a powerless non-combatant during his brother's death. He places himself right beside his brother at this fatal moment. In this novel he states that Eric had 'taken the bullet meant for his brother', demonstrating Harvey's deep sense of survivor's guilt. Eric's real death is not mentioned at all in *Comrades in Captivity*, but described in vividly imagined detail here. It seems this event was something that Harvey could only approach through fiction. In reality it was too painful.

Other characters seem to be purely from Harvey's imagination. There is no known basis in reality for the gypsy girl – known only as 'Gypsy' – or any of the characters associated with her. Mrs. Bransbury-Stuart, the married woman his character has an affair with, also seems to have been an invention.

These two women are possibly allegories for different aspects of England itself. Mrs Bransbury-Stuart is the materialistic wife of an industrialist, and uses men for her own means and then discards them, seeming to personify the industrial England that Harvey calls a 'fretful, profiteering, foolish, feverish place'. Conversely, the gypsy girl represents his ideal 'England of quiet lives, and misty orchards' in her purity, and with her knowledge of and love for the countryside. He claims that his idealised vision of England is the only England worth fighting for, and thus this brave woman who represents it overcomes the obstacles of her gender to do just that. Harvey saw the war as an opportunity for a rebirth of English society, what he called 'a New England', free from social and economic inequalities.[12] Believing that the war would bring about social revolution was what carried him through its hardships, just as the gypsy girl struggles through in the novel.

The setting for the affair with Mrs Bransbury-Stuart is based in reality. Following his certification as a solicitor, Harvey began working and living in Chesterfield, Derbyshire. At the time, Chesterfield had become a coal-mining town, and it is represented here by the fictional 'Eccleton'. His correspondence shows that he fell into depression there and hated his work so much that he quit unexpectedly in April 1914, leaving so suddenly that he abandoned his coat in the office.[13] He seems to have gone on a walking tour subsequently.[14] He found a new vocation in August when he joined the army.

Throughout the novel, Will and Eric remain privates in the Gloucestershire Regiment. In reality, both enlisted initially in the ranks and eventually received commissions (as did their brother, Roy, while their sister Gladys worked as a nurse). Eric initially joined the army with his brothers in August 1914. As in the novel, he was temporarily discharged due to family hardship reasons. In reality, this was so he could to return to look after the estate of the family farm following the death their youngest brother, Bernard, in a motorcycle accident. During this time he also completed his studies at Oxford, and thus received a commission on his return to the army, eventually reaching the rank of captain.[15] F.W. Harvey deployed with 1/5th Gloucesters to France in April 1915, earning a reputation as a scout, just as he does in the novel. In reality, he was promoted to lance corporal in recognition of this. As in the novel, he received the DCM following a night patrol that saw the destruction of an enemy listening post. The patrol was led by Lance Sergeant Raymond Knight, who is mentioned briefly in the novel. Knight and Harvey both received DCMs, and both were sent to England to receive commissions. The newly commissioned second lieutenants returned to the front in mid-1916; Knight would be killed on 22 July and Harvey captured on 16 August.

The final adventure of the novel concerns Will Harvey's escape from Germany to Holland. The character is used as a forced labourer, as was the accepted practice for prisoners from the other ranks. Aside from the obvious economic benefits for the captors, the long work days also gave the men little time to plan for escape. Conversely, officers were exempt from this forced labour, and were instead held in all-officer prison camps. Largely left alone by their guards, they had ample time to plan a getaway. This was Harvey's condition in real life. Though he did attempt escape, he was unsuccessful, and was only able to return home at the war's end. He is kinder to his character in allowing him to make it across the border.

As he suggests in his Author's Note, this novel was Harvey's attempt to explore themes of youth and war through the eyes of a fictional character. This allowed him to move freely between reality and fiction while telling his story – not to tell the facts of his experience, but in a way to present his truth.

James Grant Repshire
F.W. Harvey Doctoral Researcher
University of Exeter

Notes

1   Letter from Marion Scott to F.W. Harvey, 20 October 1925, Gloucestershire Archives (henceforth GA), F.W. Harvey Collection (henceforth FWH) D12912/1/2/89.

2   Letter from N.F. Nicholas to F.W. Harvey, 19 July 1937, GA, FWH, D12912/1/4/149.

3   E.B. Osborn, 'Trench Journals', *The Times Literary Supplement*, 12 October 1916, 769, *The Times Literary Supplement* Historical Archive online (accessed 5 April 2013).

4   F.W. Harvey, *Ducks, and Other Verse* (London: Sidgwick & Jackson Ltd, 1919) pp. 73–5.
5   The DCM was an award for valour for members of the other ranks, second only to the Victoria Cross.
6   Letter from N.F. Nicholas to F.W. Harvey, February–September 1935, GA, FWH, D12912/1/4/140.
7   Nicholas to Harvey, 19 July 1937, GA, FWH, D12912/1/4/149.
8   Letter from Marion Scott to F.W. Harvey, 26 December 1937, GA, FWH, D12912/1/2/90.
9   The Military Cross was, at the time, a third-level award for valour, awarded only to officers holding the rank of captain or below. The Bar represented a second award of the same medal.
10 Letter from Matilda Harvey to F.W. Harvey, 17 October 1918, GA, FWH, D12912/1/1/70.
11 F.W. Harvey, *Comrades in Captivity: A Record of Life in Seven German Prison Camps* (Coleford: Douglas McLean Publishing, 2010; originally Sidgwick & Jackson Ltd, 1920) p. 51.
12 Harvey, *Ducks*, pp. 73–5.
13 Letter from John Rawcliffe to F.W. Harvey, 6 May 1914, GA, FWH, D12912/1/5/10.
14 Rawcliffe to Harvey, 6 May 1914, GA, FWH, D12912/1/5/10.
15 Anthony Boden, *F.W. Harvey: Soldier, Poet* (Stroud: Alan Sutton Publishing Ltd, 1998) pp. 52–3.

BIOGRAPHICAL NOTE

Frederick William Harvey, known as 'Will' to family and friends, was born in Hartpury, Gloucestershire, on 26 March 1888. His parents were Howard Harvey, a successful horse trader, and Cecelia Matilda Harvey (*née* Waters). Shortly after Will's birth his father purchased an estate in Minsterworth, which he named The Redlands. It was at The Redlands that Will spent his formative years learning to love the Gloucestershire countryside. Will was followed by three brothers, Eric, Roy and Bernard, and a sister, Gladys. He was educated as a 'day boy' at the King's School, Gloucester, and then attended the Rossall School in Lancashire as a boarder. Following this, he was articled as a solicitor's clerk to Frank Treasure Esq of Gloucester, to begin qualifications as a lawyer. However, his heart was not in the law, but rather in the love of poetry, and he therefore did not apply himself to his studies and thus failed his exams in 1911. His family then sent him to an intensive law course at Lincoln's Inn Fields, London, where he qualified as a solicitor in 1912. He then began to practise law, though he never fully embraced the vocation.

At the outbreak of the First World War, he enlisted in Gloucester's Territorial Force battalion, 1/5th Battalion of the Gloucestershire Regiment. He arrived in France with the battalion in April 1915. In the 1/5th he became a founder of the first of the famous British trench journals, the *5th Gloucester Gazette*, which eventually brought his poetry to national attention. Serving in the infantry, he often volunteered for night patrols into no-man's-land, earning a reputation as a scout and promotion to lance corporal. In August 1915, he was awarded the Distinguished Conduct Medal, after a night patrol that saw the destruction of an enemy listening post.

He was recommended for a commission, which he received. Now a second lieutenant, he returned to England for several months of officer training. During this time he arranged publication of his first poetry collection, *A Gloucestershire Lad at Home and Abroad*, published in September 1916.

He returned to the front with the 2/5th Battalion, Gloucestershire Regiment, in July 1916, but was captured during a solo reconnaissance of the German front line on 17 August. He spent the rest of the war in various German prisoner-of-war (POW) camps, despite attempts to escape. He continued to write poetry in confinement, and was allowed to mail home manuscripts of what would be published in September 1917 as *Gloucestershire Friends: Poems from a German Prison Camp*. He returned home from the war in February 1919, and later that year published a poetry collection titled *Ducks, and Other Verses*. In 1920 he published memoirs of his POW years titled *Comrade in Captivity*.

In 1921 he married an Irish nurse, Sarah Anne Kane, and returned to practising the law. His collection, *Farewell*, of 1921 announced his intention to leave the literary world to focus on his career in law; however, he could not contain his desire to create poetry, and in 1925 published *September and Other Poems*, followed in 1926 by *In Pillowell Woods*. As early as 1928 he began writing and performing in BBC radio programmes, and would continue to do so for the rest of his life. He also saw many successful settings of his poetry to music by his accomplished musician friends Ivor Gurney, Herbert Howells and Herbert Brewer. During the Second World War, he served in the Home Guard and worked with veterans' organisations to support local men and women serving in the military. As a solicitor, he was known primarily as a defender of the poor and downtrodden. He would rarely act for the prosecution – in part due to his disdain for the prison system – and was well known for his willingness to waive fees for those who could not afford them.

Following the war, his health began to decline quickly. Still, in 1946 a final collection of his work was published, *Gloucestershire: A Selection from the Poems of F.W. Harvey*. In the final year of his life, 1956, BBC radio recognised his contribution to English poetry with a radio programme dedicated solely to his work, titled *Sing a Song of Gloucestershire*. Harvey died on 13 February 1957, just short of his 69th birthday. He was survived by his widow

Sarah Anne, his daughter Eileen Griffiths (*née* Harvey) and son Patrick. His work continues to appear in anthologies, particularly his wartime poems 'In Flanders', 'If We Return', 'The Bugler' and his most popular poem 'Ducks'.

AUTHOR'S NOTE

All art is autobiography.

Whatever happens, happens to oneself. And whether events happen in the flesh or in the soul; they happen.

This is small satisfaction to the scandal-lovers, but it is all that they will get from me.

For the reassurance of others, I will say that no living person has been depicted in this book, but that events (such as the Great War) have been used only as factual rivets in a story which is essentially a pondering upon life itself and not a representation of personalities or topics.

F.W. Harvey
1935

PREFACE

This is a war book. No one wants to read war books now-a-days; and I, who came through, do not want to write one. Only I cannot rest for the dead.

However we dislike it, the fact stands that for this generation the war must be the supreme historical event. For until the sacrifice is understood and justified our hands are unclean.

When it is understood there will be no need to wash. To realise is to be cleansed. No one can realise Truth without acting it.

Truth will give to each a personal responsibility for the dead and their dreams, which will not rest till it has appointed representatives worthy to carry those dreams into effect and seen that work engaged upon in letters and in spirit.

Then we may forget if we will. But then we shall not wish to forget.

Does a good Christian wish to forget the death of Christ? It is his shame and his glory. But to the bad Christian it is shame unglorified.

Therefore the war must be obsession to all; and until we have realised it, it will be a shameful one.

Will Harvey

PUBLISHER'S NOTE

We have endeavoured to present this book as true to its original form as possible. By reproducing the text as it was intended, we have tried our best not to interfere with the author's voice.

PART I

CHILDHOOD

CHAPTER I

'Will ye give us a glass of wine?
We be the English soldiers
We'll not give ye a glass of wine
For we be the Roman soldiers.'

Deep and ancient, that pond which never in living memory had failed, was now cleaned out by four bare-footed men.

Their necks and arms were brown as all Gloucestershire in that drought, but their uncovered shins shone curiously pale above feet caked ebony in the mud which fitted like high boots.

Thrice a day this footwear was removed by washing in water almost as black, and rubbing with rushes which alone of growing things retained a natural greenness.

Then trooping, dark-skinned and bare-footed like Moslems to a mosque, those workers entered the slight flickering shade of willows to eat heartily and hand around in an immemorial ritual the tart cool cider in a pot of horn.

The poor cattle bellowed piteously in meadows for water which had to be carried to them in buckets yoked to the shoulders of the cowman.

It was the year when Timmy Taylor returning alone to his yellow-windowed cottage a little later than his wont, was met in the moonlight by rats – thousands he said – marching to the river. They were going resolutely. Their tails (he averred) were cocked, and their little light-filled eyes fastened upon him without fear. At sight of their teeth, he who was but a quiet little mouse of a man had fled. They were many and maniac.

Timmy Taylor was one of the men who had helped dig out the big pool. His mates were Sam Bridges, Charlie Freeman, and Bill Trigg, of whom much might be told, but alas, they and their doings must not enter this tale of other and different happenings.

Forget their humanity. Behold them as marionettes cutting black chunks of earth-cake from the bottom of a pond; wheeling that confectionery in barrows up a board, and depositing it in one long heap, shaped like a low swede-pile, upon the bank ...

That fertile mud, accepting from all vagrant winds the various pollen they bore and scattered, chose to rear that only that it desired.

Two years later it was invisible in an army of rank and nodding nettles sprung to the height of a man's head. And there in a daisied meadow drowsed in shadow of those nettles a nursemaid with but one leg; and by her, a little boy.

In days when bobbed hair was not a fashion hers had been cut short, making a dark oblong frame to a pale rather oval face. She had black expressionless eyes like plums in a pudding – but it was Christmas pudding, which he liked. To look at her you would say that she was town-bred, though in fact she was not.

He was five years old. She was eighteen or nineteen – but what does that signify? She was 'grown up' like his mother whose age and stead-fastness was that of the blue Cotswolds. Years mean nothing to a child, and where it otherwise girls of eighteen are not all of the same age.

Her name? She was called Clemmy. She lay stretched in the buttercups of the meadow, her crutch near by hidden by them and big daisies.

She was telling him a story which concerned a giant so big that his eyes were troubled with the stars as ours are with sparks when we look out of a train in a tunnel – which we should not do because it is dangerous; only sometimes ... The boy nodded. Sometimes dangerous things were nice.

And the clouds caught in the giant's beard like cobwebs. Yes, Tom Freeman had pulled down cobwebs from the stable to put on a horse that was bleeding. If you should cut a finger, sticky cobwebs stopped the blood from coming out of it.

Her companion supposed that Clemmy had used them when her leg was cut off. But he said nothing. She was always cross if he mentioned her 'other leg'.

The swallows chased across the water hunting flies. Their backs were blue: their breasts flame-coloured in the low sun.

Fe, Fi, Fo, Fum! thundered the voice of the giant. He had made a dinner of little boys. But Jack who was only a little boy (like himself) had killed that monster.

Brave Jack! If only he, Willie, could kill a giant ... 'Soldiers, Clemmy,' he cried, 'let's have soldiers.' And then Clemmy began the ritual of her favourite game by singing in a deep clear tone the words which stand at the head of this chapter –

Will ye give us a glass of wine? We be the English soldiers.

The boy's eyes brightened like little stars. But, 'not yet, Clemmy!' he pleaded, 'not now.' And the nursemaid conceded the point in favour of peace.

Yes, we'll give ye a glass of wine, For we be English soldiers.

Then again she repeated in song her request on behalf of the warriors for alcoholic refreshment. And this time the answer was defiant:

'We'll not give ye a glass of wine,
For we be the Roman soldiers.'

At that with heightened colour the child seizing a sword fashioned kindly and roughly out of thatching sticks by Bill Trigg advanced gold-shod through buttercups upon the hill of nettles; and a queer smile curved the girl's lips.

A fierce battle ensued in which bare legs were blistered – aye and cheeks and arms, and tall nettles lowered with blows. Still the girl smiled and watched,

Then after a wile, satisfied perhaps that small calves had been sufficiently stung, or fearing possibly a scarcity of foes for the morrow – 'Willie', she called.

'Willie!'

He came obediently as was his custom: he always obeyed Clemmy. And though she frightened him; fear was not the motive of that obedience. Differently to his mother, but in some sure way he loved her.

He pitied her besides, and hated her foes. Those Roman soldiers (this was his interpretation of the song which she alone sang) had cut off Clemmy's leg!

He could not know that her bodily affliction was the result of a medical operation – the removal of diseased bone consequent upon consumption. Still less could he have been expected to guess his lady to be a feebly perverted, but alas! imaginative girl.

Bred in the open air, the little boy was a loyal and stout-hearted champion. Nor was his knight-errantry play, still less pose.

The brave and glittering stories of Malory he had never heard. Stevenson's charming *Child's Garden* would not have appealed to him. He scorned all fire-lit fancy-fed games of the nursery unaccompanied by hurt. Hans Anderson, read to him by his mother, he loved; but not 'The brave tin Soldier,' for he could not believe in his existence.

It is the plain fact that his childhood was not that happy poetic period generally believed in. Even so early he had discovered that one must suffer for one's beliefs, and did so joyously in the games which were his life.

Then even, the thirst (the curse, but inspiration) of his life, which never left him even when he grew up, was for reality:– for true adventure: adventure with Life. He preferred the strings of the nettle to any soft fire-lit play.

'Willie!'

Having kissed him, Clemmy gathered her crutch and got up, hobbling towards the farm house, till remembering something –

'Eric!' she called.

Then another tiny figure, in petticoats, arose from the grass and followed. It was Willie's brother, her second charge whom she had forgotten.

CHAPTER II

'My father bred great horses,
Chestnut, grey and brown.
They grazed about the meadow,
And trampled into town.
They left the homely meadows
And trampled far away,
The great shining horses
Chestnut, and brown, and grey.
Gone are the horses
That my father bred
And who knows whither? ...
Or whether starved or fed? ...
Gone are the horses;
And my father's dead.'

Not long after this Clemmy was dismissed, and passes out of the story. She had fulfilled her destiny in their life of one small boy.

He shed a few tears at her going; but Eric was not inclined to weep or rejoice. Younger by two years than Willie, be continued absorbed in quiet mysterious little games, and a soft and brooding innocence. Clemmy's spell had never fallen over his babyhood, nor changed his play with daisies for war with nettles.

Life is a time of quick forgetting; and childhood very swiftly filled in with new experience. Other strange happenings overgrew the gap made by Clemmy's departure. For instance Sam 'got hurted' ... That was the phrase Willie heard uttered hoarsely in the half-light of a September morning – and then, 'Mustard, he done it zur – the big chestnut.'

His father and mother were dressing. Eric was in the cot near by; and he, since he resolutely refused to lie elsewhere, in the big bed. Several months before he had been given a separate room, and for a week his parents were roused in the dead of night by the same small

white figure scrambling into their bed. Smacking proved as ineffec-
tual as reproof. The room allotted was in a distant part of the house,
and since the child's persistent journey in pitch darkness was along
a passage which crossed two flights of steep stairs, it was considered
wise to reinstate him, and a cot was procured for Eric.

So on the morning in question Willie was awakened by a sharp
rattle of gravel upon the window, and heard his father informed of
Sam's accident in the words already set down.

His father immediately went out of the bedroom, and his mother
although incompletely dressed slipped a shawl around her shoulders
and followed.

This was queer. Willie's curiosity was not less than normal. It was
he who had startled a congregation the Sunday before by following
the Rector's stentorian 'Get thee behind me Satan!' with the shrill
question 'And what did he do when he got behind him?' Willie got up.

Descending the front stairs, still in his nightdress, he came to the
foot in time to see a man carried in on a stable-door by four workmen, and deposited gently upon the dining-room sofa. His father
followed, directing, and his mother was fetching something in a glass
for the man to drink.

Creeping unnoticed into the room Willie saw that the man on the
sofa was Sam, and that Sam's face was white and puckered.

Willie laughed at the funny noise Sam made (it was like a cow
talking to herself) and then he was noticed. His mother carried him
upstairs and scolded him for coming down, and very severely for
laughing when the man groaned. Poor Sam was hurt. He knew that.
He did not want to laugh at the funny sound, yet in the memory of it
he laughed again.

His mother was surprised and frightened at this callousness. Had
he been other than her own little son she would have suspected him
of a bad nature. As it was she absolved him, and looked to herself
for the root of the mischief. Yet she had never been cruel – beautiful
unselfish woman.

Later she discovered that many unaccountable things in childhood
which can neither be chastised nor prayed away do of their own
accord go. For a child lives lives not his, and not his mother's, ere he
lives his own.

That little laugh troubled her many a night. She prayed that her
child might not grow up cruel. Cruelty was to her strong kind nature

something worse than other sins; a blacker (since a meaner and weaker) transgression than any reckless breaking of the commandments from one to ten.

In his babyhood she had cried bitterly on first discovering that pulsing of the brain discernible through the pulp of any tiny half-knit skull. God, has she borne an idiot? Now she grieved lest her darling should turn out to be a monster. Such it is to be a mother, such, though in a lesser intensity, is it (as artists know – and soldiers) to love anything that one has created through suffering and glory ...

Meanwhile Willie, in bed, reflected upon everything except his conduct. The big fiery-tempered Mustard had kicked Sam, and broken his leg. Perhaps he would now have only one – like Clemmy – and the trees. Trees had one leg only though hundreds of arms. Trees stood still, but Clemmy walked. Perhaps Sam had kicked Mustard, just as Mustard had kicked Sam. This thought, which amused him, he mentioned later to Sam's fellow workmen who then gazed at one another with amused faces while Bill Trigg said he was 'dazed if this buoy o' master's' hadn't 'got a yud on him', adding that Sam 'orter bin a cowman.'

Sam was not good with horses. Nervous himself he made them nervously restive. Then he got frightened and beat them to the accompaniment of curses and a stamping clatter of iron horse-shoes, which awoke Willie on market mornings and called down rebuke from his father who was dressing at a window overlooking the yard. (The reader has perhaps guessed that Willie's father was a horse breeder and farmer.) The child lay dreaming. A little tapping of ivy and Virginia creeper mimicked the multitudinous clatter of hooves as a string of great shining animals tramped off to market tethered head and tail with side-lines.

Sunlight streamed further into the room awaking Eric. Presently Mother came in to dress the boys. Prayers were prolonged by a tender little sermon to the elder on kindness, to people and to beasts. Then both children went down to play with floating islands of brown-sugared porridge until that edible fairyland had disappeared, swallowed up by giants.

Breakfast over, they were cautioned not to go near the stables, warned especially against the bull in a small meadow near by, and turned loose upon the island – that is the farm – which was their world.

They saw Bill Trigg harnessing Buttercup to a spring cart, and noticing the two ladders and a pyramid of wicker pots near by, concluded rightly that the little plum orchard was to be picked, and at once attached themselves to the party.

Neither Buttercup nor Bill Trigg can be dismissed in a sentence, even if one wanted to. Buttercup had been in her day a hunter and steeplechaser – but that day was twenty years past. She had gained shining cups that now reflected themselves in the dining-room side-board, and her owner (note that I have avoided the word master) would as soon have cast those bright trophies on a dung-heap as have sold the old yellow mare.

She was, though stiff, full of inbred race and temperament. A man or a woman might ride her, but never a fool. She held, and had always held, her own ideas as to the rushing of fences. 'Lay your hands down, sit back, and leave me alone' had been the principle of her mettlesome days, which hardened as she grew, older, and hoarded her experience. She would carry you (if you were fit to be carried) through a day's hunting as well and better than horses half or a quarter her age. But you must leave her to do it.

Now, a little tired of gazing in pools at the reflection of an old stiff horse feeding in meadows less green; in sunshine less warm than it used to be, she found it (doubtless) refreshing to reach, when requested, a helping hoof to those who appreciated her – to take part in such menial tasks as these.

Bill Trigg, though he could not be said to rival in breeding the aristocracy of Buttercup, yet suggested by his appearance Frederick William the Great, grown poor and honest. His side whiskers, his despotism ... But he was built on a rather smaller plan than was the old emperor: and he wore corduroys.

A reprobate juicy old man ... He loved the children. And the children rather liked him.

He had served their grandpa, and having (he proclaimed) helped 'Master Howard' through many a youthful scrape, was permitted to do his own jobs in his own way even when that way was not wholly to his master's liking.

'Kim oop!' he cried to Buttercup, and the old mare moved daintily forward with the load of hampers and ladders.

Entering the orchard with the two little boys following, Bill, Buttercup, and Timmy Taylor who had joined them, stopped: ladders were propped against trees: the mare unharnessed to graze; and the fruit-picking begun.

Eric quietly seated himself in dappled grass to play, and to eat the fallen plums. Willie followed Bill Trigg up a ladder to do the same, and to put questions concerning things in general which provoked a voluble reminiscence in the jovial old picker.

'Are the wasps flies?'

'Wasps', said Bill evading the question, 'was the little baggers with hot feet – and don't 'e forget it.' Willie, like the unskilful debated, was side-tracked on to this new argument. He did not believe that wasps' feet were hot. Clemmy had shown him a wasp killing a fly. After he had killed it, Clemmy had killed the wasp, and made the wasp work his sting too, and the sting was in his tail.

Clemmy, answered Bill, was a bitch

'A what?'

If Willie didn't believe that there about wasps' feet could let one stand on him ver a while.

Willie wouldn't.

Why were wasps' feet hot then?

Why, from using 'em too much, an' walking sideways up windows and back'ard head down over ceilings and such. Willie had only to walk back'ard head down on a ceiling to find out for himself.

'I know where a wasp nest is,' interjected Willie, ignoring the impossible challenge.

Wasp-nestes! – Bill had taken hundreds, thousand on 'em.

'What for?'

To sell their maggots in Gloucester, and to fishermen. This entailed an explanation (derided by Willie) that a wasp's young 'uns wer grubs, and good to bait hooks with because fish like eating them (yutting 'em).

Bill passed on to wasps' houses which were of brown paper 'made special by the wasps themselves' out of 'bark and stuff', and shaped into hundreds of cells, or cradles for the babies ...

'They'll make 'em anywhere a'most.'

'The one I know of is in a bank,' volunteered Willie – 'by the black-berry bushes, over the pond.'

'Aye, they most an' generally goes there,' agreed the old man, 'but I've knowed 'em in very queer places, where a man mon 'oudn't expect 'em to be nohow. Thee dost know old John Helps the cider maker: zees un in church a Zunday I warn't, Well, he did find a nest in a queer place. Five years ago last fall a was making sweet some old barr'ls and hogsheads fer the new drink which were uncommon plenteous, so as they had to pull out from the back of a shed all the old extra casks fer to hold it. Well, they was a rolling of these 'ere out, and a rinsing of 'em; and John, a wer sat over the bung-hole o' the last ready to stave in the end on't – when what? A feels a prick in the seat of his trousers. A gets up. Out comes the wasps buzzing angry at bein' rolled about, and all their babies made giddy. Everybody run. But old John didn't run. What'd he do? He sat down again on the hole. 'I'll be stung in one place,' he says, 'not everywhere!' The old mon said that; and 'bring a bung,' says he, hardly wriggling, 'and we'll lock 'em up' – 'Tyunt reasonable,' says he, 'to give liberty to wasps as have been treated as these 'uns have. Human beings wouldn't stand it neither.'

So we brings a bung – a big un, and shapes un slantwise so as to fit in any hole, and as soon as old John gets up Bang! In a goes. And there was a cask full o' raging captives. 'Whop! Old John's hand claps his behind and there lies a cluster of forty wasps as had bin a-hanging on to him head downward by their tails.

'Aha!' shouted Willie, 'I knew 't wasn't their feet.'

'Bist a smart monkey bisn't?' replied Bill. 'Down thee goes! I wants fer to shift this ladder round a bit.'

'What happened to the wasps in the cask?' asked the child descending.

'Left 'em there,' was the answer, 'and there they be now fer aal I knows – starved to death, or yutting one another.'

'But where be young Eric?' enquired the narrator, looking round as he stepped off the ladder, 'you'd best go and find 'ee, else e'll be getting into summat.'

But where was Eric? Timmy Taylor had seen him toddling off in the direction of the farm (he thought) 'to find his mam'. They left it at that; but on returning an hour later for the cider which had been forgotten, they found that no one there had tidings of him.

'Drat the bwoys,' cried Trigg. He added that it was a wonder as their poor mother didn't jump up in the air and never come down.

But where was Eric?

The servants had not seen him in the house. The workmen had not seen him outside. His name was cried through all the rooms, the farm buildings, and the Barn.

Then a single cry of astonishment and alarm directed the searchers to a stable, and peering over the half door they beheld at first a darkness, then 'Mustard' the huge chestnut cart-horse who had kicked Sam, and lastly, embracing the hocks of this irritable and exasperated beast, a tiny figure crooning to himself and the animal a little song. It was Eric. They called to him in whispers to come away. And Eric came – reluctantly.

Then 'Damn us all!' cried Trigg, touching his hat to Mrs. Harvey, to indicate that the oath carried no disrespect – 'Damn us all! this 'un must be a soldier. Nothing won't harm 'ee 'tis certain. Make 'un a brave soldier ma'am. No bullet with kill 'ee!'

But – Bill Trigg lied.

CHAPTER III

It is necessary to hurry on. But there are things which must be said.

The farm lay in Severn Valley; a region of rich, well-fruited land, attached to a city famous in history, inhabited first by the little long-headed dark Iberians; built, destroyed and rebuilded again and again. Caer Glow, Glevum, Gloucester – call it what you will – it had echoed the tragedies and the comedies of a thousand years of rich life.

Tall and bright; like a lily in the hands of Morning – the tower of its exquisite and enduring cathedral dominated for a surrounding ten miles the low meadows, and influenced powerfully, if in diverse ways, the thoughts of those who worked therein.

Its chimes were perhaps a call to God; perhaps a ringing from faery, a call to bait, a musical snore of the church, a floating heaven-dropped word to conscience, a hail to the rustic Whittington eager of success, a solace to such (alike weary) as had found, or failed to find that bauble, a renunciation of sin, an invitation to it.

It stood, to some, for escape; to some, for sweet content. A beacon-fire of Christ: a beacon-blaze of the devil – all things to all men; there it stood!

Beyond it the high Cotswolds, scarred white with quarries, and enveloped in mist like the bloom on the ripened plums, stretched mile after mile in sharp though shadowed outline ...

Such, on one coast was the ocean of influence (for it is with influences that a novelist is concerned) surrounding that farm which has been spoken of, with deliberation, as an island.

On other sides, the royal Forest of Dene, the Cherry-country, and the Bristol Channel, lisped round or sang like seas near or remote their songs of strangeness and romance to marooned inhabitants.

The isle was one of a few outlying upon the village of Minsterworth, whose name sufficiently explains its ancient usage as the worth or farm of the monks at Gloucester – a parish consisting mainly of riverside pasture subject on passing into private ownership to many strange species of tithe since commuted to monetary value.

The inhabitants of this pastoral island (known to surveyors as Maycote farm) numbered about a dozen souls living in close contact. Foraging expeditions were made almost daily by the master whose business strategy was to dispose of rough 'two year olds' to Cotswold farmers, who trained them to work, and sold them back at the profit a couple of years later. These fully grown and well disciplined horses then proceeded to fatten themselves on Minsterworth pasture prior to being sold to Breweries, Corporations, Railways and so forth.

Without keeping an elaborated system of books, the memory of Willie's father regarding animals, and his knowledge of what they would have grown into in given spaces of time, was so dependable, that in receiving a prospective buyer's demand for so many 'pitters' 'vanners' 'shunters' or brewery horses, he could always locate, procure, and sell them to him – at a profit.

Everybody was pleased – the farmer who had got two years work, and ten pounds above what he spent, the buyer who had only to write saying what kind of horses he wanted, to get it; and the dealer who on a single animal had earned two profits by expert knowledge.

Horse dealers have a bad name, and some deserve it, but it would be hard to discover a trade or profession which so prosecuted united better a personal profit with the general interest in days when horses were of national importance.

Willie's father was ostensibly selling horse-flesh – and so by common inference, buyers; but what he actually sold was a very personal skill and judgement which was profitable to all concerned.

Do the learned professions always do so much?

On top of this he was supplying his island with life and the means of living it naturally and wholesomely in companionship that only Shakespeare could fully appreciate.

To the sceptical (maddened with the life of modern cities) it may be remarked that there were on that island degrees, but no differences – and no poverty! The horrible separation of kind, so common with them, was unknown to these. A mellow humanity rather than any remnants of the feudal system, which at its best served the same turn, (those with knowledge will admit the truth of that statement) made each responsible for all.

Another distinction between that life and the accepted travesty of life in crowded cities was the permanent possibility of solitary adventure; and indeed the possibility of being solitary at all.

Adventure may be actual, or imaginary; it may affect the flesh or the spirit: and it is this latter kind which is of the greater potency to make and to mould character.

The following may stand as a type of spiritual adventure and shall be related in Willie's own words – written years after in the heart-breaking time when he was trying to live by his pen – honestly. (The difficulty, good people, lies simply in that last word; as the sting of the wasp lies in its tail!)

That the big-little adventure was considered unfit for publication, and in fact refused by no less than eight editors, is a reason neither for nor against its inclusion as a colour in this larger picture where it illustrates better than anything else the ting with which we are at present chiefly concerned – namely, the atmosphere which surrounded and influenced the childhood of these two little beings.

That is all right. The fault to be found with it is none of those enumerated by the refusing editors – lack of plot, oddness, tenuity, and so forth.

The fault is rather this: that Willie, remembering his childhood's strange experience and writing it down years after despaired of acceptable explanations (as if they were necessary!) and sank here and there into the cowardice of attempting a justification though only by allusion to minds sophisticated – with which minds his own had become numbered.

He felt (one suspects) a desire to justify the tale – the truth – not only to others, but even to himself!

This is 'the contagion of the world's slow slow stain.'

The important point is that what Willie attempted to describe was something that actually occurred to him. From which let no reader conclude that Willie was an abnormal child.

He was an ordinary, country-bred, healthy, little boy fallen in circumstances as nearly perfect as is possible in this age (or perhaps in any other) for living his own healthy little life.

He was abnormal only in the sense that all children would be if so bred, and given liberty to discover with their own eyes the sleeping beauty of the world.

That terrifying Beauty which at the touch of genius from time to time has turned uneasily in her slumber, never yet has awakened to look with clear eyes upon us men, and cause us to gaze back into her own.

Maybe she will never do so, yet in that is our hope, undying through all aeons of years – our one hope.

That is a single interpretation. Maybe it was the vision of Beauty to be awakened in the world. Maybe it was a child's perception of something far different lying in the heart of nature and awaiting its hour. Reply it was both. Willie never discovered what it was. Only it happened. It happened so.

CHAPTER IV

A few words of Mr. and Mrs. Harvey – parents of these boys. (Patience! I know what you want. There shall be 'action' enough presently!)

Let it be stated at once that save as large kind impersonal forces, the children at this time knew little of them.

Yet had these two people died (as one did) before their personalities had been explored and recorded in the memories of their children, their influence would still have been a large thing in their lives.

Personality is often exaggerated. It is, in truth, but the fascinating divergence of mankind. Humanity is the great river running steadily through.

Though the differences of men is their interest, it is their sameness which is divine. Our great mother – the Earth – what comparison of difference is permitted to her? Yet she is beloved of her children whom she feeds and takes to her breast.

So humanity, though broad and impersonal, is God-like. Humanity is an influence. Personality is but an interest.

Yet as this story is not (alas!) for babes whose desire is 'Father', and 'Mother', but for grown-ups, thinking in terms of Mr. and Mrs. Harvey; more must be revealed to them than the children themselves knew, or ever wanted to know.

Howard Harvey was the third son of a large farmer of the country who, starting poorly, had laid field to field and built barns after the fashion of the man in the Bible – but honestly, and by dint of something more than a cold perseverance, for his industry was hot iron sweating sparks to kindle things around with a similar heat, rather than steel cutting a path for itself.

It was said that he was ambitious. But a closer investigation shows that his 'ambition' was to drive a horse which could be passed by nothing upon the road prior to the days of bicycles and motors – always referred to indiscriminately as 'those damned things.'

This ambition was easily attained. His later success was due rather to 'something spontaneous and pushing in his inside,' which combined with a genuine capacity for farming and managing land.

The hard times were not over when his children were boys, and Howard, with the rest, had to work hard, developing a natural industry under the dynamic energy of the old man.

That wonderful force acting through environments and also through heredity was transmitted to bodily frames less sturdy than his own in those of his sons, who wore out while the generator of it, and then, lived hardily on, a 'character' – almost a landmark of the country.

That towering rustic figure of eighty years; the tall white hat black-banded in perpetual mourning for its predecessors; the paunch directing attention to its unvarying cover of moleskin crossed with long gold links of a watch-chain; the short brown cloth gaiters worn to shield the trousers; the five foot holly-stick which made a crutch for the thumb of his right hand; these were known at every fair throughout the country, and to grand-children whose fathers were already in their graves, exhausted by the restless energy of this old man.

And the same fire of vitality then flickering in him; quenched already in two of his sons, flamed out again in the third generation.

Take away your tables of genealogy, burn your Burkes! This, or nothing, is all that is meant by good breeding. And you – the little scientific know-alls, forbear to talk in your damned superior fashion of Mendel and his law which anyway you don't understand! Listen merely for once and you shall hear what is more convincing than your generalities, namely, that both children and grandchildren of this old man were in every way (save one) totally different to one another and to him, and that this common factor was to be found Where? – in an original dynamic energy transmitted by one man. This energy which was one, diversified itself in its application under other minds. Thus we come to Howard. Now, what was his ambition? That question can be answered shortly – his wife and his children. His method of providing for them has already been dealt with.

Howard was as unlike his father as could well be imagined. Substitute for the great bluff farmer a small though sturdy figure; for the round ruddy countenance a lined face – strong but a little anxious; change the forceful overbearing disposition to one of extreme gentleness; the temper ever liable to flare in short-lived violence, to a steady brilliance of courage. Substitute the broad boisterous man's humour with a child's twinkling gaiety. Keep only the unresting energy which is wearing out its sheath in a high-strung nature; and there, nervously gnawing his moustache even when playing at cricket with his boys, home for the holidays – there you have him.

Perhaps nothing could better show the difference between the two men than the fact that he did play cricket with his children. Imagine the old man ever doing it. What! The young varmints should be out at work! Only the tearful pleadings of their mother procured for them the small education they obtained. And she paid for it. Leisure!

Howard remembered his own hard boyhood; and the sins of the fathers had this beneficial result, that they made him determined that such should not be visited upon the children to the third or fourth generation if he could help it.

No man was ever luckier in choosing a wife. Miss Waters, the daughter of a prosperous farmer in an adjoining county was one of those remarkable characters of which life shows more than books – and life few enough.

The reason is simple.

Good women are notoriously hard 'to draw'.

This dark girl was a white magic against misfortune; a soothing finger upon all trembling evil strings … And her power increased as she grew older.

Anyone seeing her at the age of forty would have seen a rather far country-woman with a magnificent head. Having spoken to her he would have said, 'a kind person'. Knowing her well he would have called her 'a true saint'; – and so damned her.

For it is the misfortune of this age that nobody believes in saints, and that the word 'good' means 'too good'. Very well then – she was 'awfully jolly.'

She was good as the green earth is good, rather than as the yellow district visitor whose mouth is shaped to utter prunes and prisms – albeit biblical prunes, and prisms most holy.

And now gentle reader – if any – I will tell you (since it will take no more than a few seconds) why you sicken at the word 'good', and so, incidentally, put me to an unnecessary trouble.

It is for three reasons. Firstly, because the Victorians caused it to mean something it should not have meant – and never did mean.

Secondly, because you think more of words than of things which lie behind them. And thirdly, because (pardon, gentle reader) you are a fool.

And with the same condescension, brother artist, I will tell you why your figures, and mine, are such measly little puppets. It is because virtue is too hard to draw, and too big.

Take Mrs. Harvey. Add to goodness, the calmness, the strength, the sweetness of old earth; perceive rather, that these are all included in it. What siege even of old age and disease can carry dramatic terror into that castle of nobleness? The outer faculties fallen, the senses dim, what can destiny put to reign over the inner court of wild flowers and perennial sunshine?

How is art's little edging of line, and so careful disposition of light and shade to accomplish it, tell me?

I have said she was a good woman. Music may hint the meaning of that; still better perhaps, wild flowers, a nosegay of dark violets in spring; and later on, twined honeysuckle and old man's beard. That was the effect she had on people.

Must I sink to the level of your popular novelist and tell you the shape of her nose, and what she wore? Very well, it was an English nose, and her clothes were English too. The whole lot was English.

So now we can get on ... Hastily and insufficiently sketched, such were the parents of the little boys who had just been sent to school, at the time of their old grandfather's last illness, thus to a reporter described by Trigg, periodically spitting upon the sanded floor of the 'Five Alls.'

'A wer never the same since the red bull tossed 'un up. 'Twas a quiet beast, but all things do have their natur', and will till the world be drowned flat once more again. As 'a pushed horns a got savager. A chased Tater Baggit dro a hedge – a did. But most and gener'ly old Master could do anything wi' un, and so a would never believe as 'twer true. "Tater Baggit," a laughed, "Tater Baggit 'ud run, the winnocking creatur, from the crows I pays 'un to scare away, if they had the thought to craw at un all together."

I wer born too nigh a "ood to be afeared of owls" – a said. And out 'a goes, wi' his boots off too, and wearing his old red carpet slippers, to talk to the bull where a was grazing in the little paddock and scratch the curly front of his yud. And a come chuckling back. It were all right that time.

But when it come threshing season, then down at the next farm an engine starts up a-droning and a-bellowing and a-moaning, like a bee and a bull and old Sorrow all together. And believe me when the bull did hear that it put un into a fury. Maybe he thought it wer another bull ready to fight un. But whatever a thought, the maggotts o' rage crawled up into a's yud and round and round inside, and a swelled a-self out wi' angry wind, and bellowed back most wonnerful.

And as t'other bull kep' on same as before neither higher nor lower but boo-oo and moo-oo, and boo-oo again, a got madder and madder, and started to tear and paw the fence so as to get at un.

"Go and tell that damned thing to stop," said the old Master, "we'll get un in afore damage is done." Tater Baggit went off as fast as his legs 'ud take him, glad enough to be out 'ont.

Then when they stopped, and nobody did move very fast to go drive un into the yard, why the old mon steps out like a did before, when a had the red slippers on – only now twas boots, being morning. "Come! Come! my dainty!" a called. And the bull came at un like a bolting star.

Whoick! over the hedge a went. Whop! a come down. And a didn't waken for dree weekes. Then, "Bill Trigg, I bin dead," a said to me, sat by un one day, "haven't I, Bill?!"

"No, Master," I said to ee.

"But I have!"

"When men have been dead, they don't get up and talk about it," says I.

"What about Jesus Christ?" a rapped out.

"Well, thee bisn't ee," I said.

But he damned and shouted so as t'wer'nt no use argying over it wi un, and so a went till the day a died, and didn't speak no more.' Bill drank reflectively from his mug ...

'That were some while later, as ye may know. But, as I say, a wer never the same mon since. Sometimes a would go and drive round a bit wi a slow quiet 'oss, and that wer'nt like un. A took to wear a read dressing gown, but a never left off the big white chimley hat, and a used to frighten them as met him in the lanes till they got to know who 'twas.

'At last a lay in the big bed upstairs and couldn't see any o'the things a wanted to. A lay in the girt bed wi a roof on't. And I did come and tell un about the farm and the beasts and what wer wi'em.

'Master Howard, and the two little uns with their ma did come and talk to un too, but a liked me there best because I would tell 'en what had calved and what hadn't, and remind un o' them vaur cattle o' his as beat the world at the show in London; and (mind ye) the Prince o' Wales himself said as a wer proud to meet un that day. "Don't you mention it," said he modest to the Prince.

'Then one morn I came in and I seed at the foot o' the bed on the shiny pole as ran along the bottom near the window, summat as made me stare – a robin, and the old mon un throwing crumbs to un.

"Master,' I said, 'don't ee do't."

"Do what?" said he.

"Don't ee courage thic bird to come in."

'"Why, I do like to see un," he said,

"Well, I don't."

"Why?" a said then.

I up and told un, "It be a sign," I said, "a sign as somebody be going to die."

I didn't say outright as t'wer e as wer meant. That would ha made un angry. But a died that night.' Bill took another reflective sup from his replenished mug. 'Course a did,' he added.

* * *

'The deceased had for some time been ailing consequent upon injury sustained earlier in the year when he had the misfortune to be gored by one of the cattle for which he was famous as a breeder throughout the country.'

Such was the transcription of Bill's information by the reporter – Bill being illiterate.

CHAPTER V

'O fair enough are sky and plain,
But I know fairer far;
Those are as beautiful again
That in the water are.'

It will be the lot of those who read through the first portion of this history to follow the development of two boys, the characters of whose parents have been hastily and perhaps insufficiently sketched, from the atmosphere and environment of that rural existence and tradition which has occupied by reason of its paramount potency of influence the greater part of the preceding pages, into the adventure which were later on to befall them, and the world; tracing in doing so two distinct and widely different interpretations of that single energy projected by the old man whose death a reporter and Bill Trigg have described – the one in modern sixth standardised English, and the other merely in the rambling countrified tongue of William Shakespeare.

Nurtured by the parents, nourished by the country described and impelled by the dynamic force of that dead man, Willie has exhibited certain traits of character already recorded; but Eric, being two years younger, has of necessity shown but a blurred and baby outline.

This, ere the book of their early childhood is shut, must be remedied, and shall be, by means of the two following incidents both of which occurred while the boys were still running loose upon the farm just prior to their being sent to a small school.

Willie was then eight, and Eric six years of age.

But prior to a narration of these events, and in parenthesis it may avoid future argument to point out that the stream of human energy may manifest itself in activity, or in ecstacy. The same force may produce an Arctic discoverer or a contemplative mystic. It is therefore nothing to be wondered at if in the lives of these children its results are very different from those produced in the life of the grandfather from whom it is convenient to derive it, because to trace it back to God would involve considerable labour, and there is else no one so likely to accept and appreciate the compliment as that old gentleman …

The flash of two blue overalls now directs us to the green steep banks of a pond mentioned in Chapter I. As before, singing is heard. But tune and words are different. It was one of the hymns most frequently sung by the family on Sunday evenings:

'All things bright and beautiful
All creatures great and small;
All things wise and wonderful,
The Lord God – He made all.'

The bright little tune was lustily sung by the smaller of the two boys. 'I sing loud as ever I can for Jesus to hear' Eric had amused them all by saying at the end of his last drawing-room performance. The slurring of the words showed that they were familiar enough to have been almost forgotten. He sang as the Catholic prays; gabbling the syllables, and forgetting them in the firm and central 'intention' which is all that matters. In other words he was devoid of all self-consciousness. It was natural religion in the true sense of the term – so natural that, ordinarily speaking, it was not religion at all. If he worshipped (as there is no doubt he did) he did so by spontaneous combustion: because the pool was lovely, and it was a happiness to sing – none of which need have been explained had people generally any understanding of children, or of religion.

He lay on his little stomach overlooking the water, and saw beneath him the swallow-wimpled surface; the water-weeds brilliantly ravelled; and below them yellow clay, and moss shrill-green; all cleaner, brighter, clearer, than any in the air; and again beyond, and infinitely deep, an exquisite and unfamiliar sky that mirrored in every detail the one above him, but added to it a remote and spiritual beauty never captured on earth.

The attitude was symbolic for (though this is to anticipate) it was one which he never abandoned his life through. And in symbolic fashion also was it temporally broken, as broken temporally it was destined to be through life. A long-drawn squeal which ended abruptly, and was renewed with a greater intensity and ear-piercing power; that, and Willie tugging at his stocking, withdrew his ecstatic attention.

'Pig! – come on!' cried his brother, setting off towards the yard at a run. And he arose and followed.

When they reached the place which lay two fields away, the preliminary and essential business (which was slaughter) had been accomplished. A great sprawling pool of bright and clotted blood caused Eric to shudder and whiten, but both he and Willie watched as though fascinated the carcass dragged away and singed in a bright flame of straw boltens.

The black and white bristles were then scraped off; and piggy looked, and sounded when thumped, like a hollow tree. Willie hit him to find out.

A pouch-mouthed man informed them that so far as his (that is the pig's) inside was concerned it was just like a man's; also that this animal (the pig) was the only one that didn't bend his knees before going to sleep. 'Horses do, and cattle do, and a praying man do, but a pig don't'

He then pulled out yards and yards of intestine that squeaked. He told it out like a rope, and hung it over his arm. And Eric ran away.

Willie remained, though somewhat disgusted, and saw the white bladder given to Tater Baggit who had been taken on the farm after the death of his old master. And Tater and other lads, having inflated it, kicked it about the moon-lit meadows till it broke, and their play ended.

This is the first of two incidents in Eric's childhood which alike by indelible impression upon him, and in view of those subsequent events of history that are the platform from which the writer must needs survey every incident to attain unity in the story – now seem to demand record.

The other shall be shortly dealt with. It is in reality a prank played by that 'Something' which frightened and bewildered the other little boy, and it may or may not be an allegory; but it happened, and it is just as simple to understand as the other was complex.

Were it written down apart from the events of this particular story and merely (as so it might be) as an allegorical essay, it should be called – 'Truth'.

Lying in the darkness after he had gone to bed, and before he slept, Eric hated to feel any strange thing touch him. His whole nature funked it. Fear is generally the mother of anger, and it made him angry when a moth brushed his face with blundering wings. He wanted to kill it. That is just what happened on this particular night.

He lighted the candle and raised his hand. The moth remained quite still upon the pillow. Its two fan-like wings were extended and he noticed how precisely and beautifully they were barred. Only the two antennae kept swaying a little like branches in a wind.

PART II

SCHOOL DAYS

CHAPTER I

There is no subject upon which a writer can more easily and pleasurably 'spread himself' than – school days. Viewed retrospectively, here are high spirits, high hopes, inexperience, and adventure, standing enhanced in a haze of sentiment:– all the media of popular success. But we are concerned with the telling of a story.

What, seen solely from the story's point of view, was the influence of that time upon the characters of these two boys?

The time was seven years. Ask the boys themselves and they would say – or rather have said – that it was the most important period of their lives. That means that they were more conscious of its influences – good and bad – than of any before or since. It means merely that.

From the observer's standpoint – that is, from the view of their mother, the author, and the reader – what took place?

There took place a change in play, in manners, and in codes of 'honour' – the latter, in inverted commas!

Games, speech, and certain habits, were not different, but what (ask their mother), what underneath had altered? ...

Breeding, and the first and freshest environment had done their work. Underneath the new games, the fresh habits, the revised vocabulary, the boys were the same. Mothers only will appreciate how much.

Their experience had merely made them – themselves. Only more so. Superficially they were absolutely different. Essentially, all that had happened to them was a hardening and developing of characteristics already their own.

Were it not for that hardening and that developing, this book would hold no account at all of their school-days.

These lucky little boys never had a governess: moreover the first school they went to wasn't one. It was a spinster lady who kept house for her bachelor brother at an adjoining farm and found the time dull; and they were her only pupils.

She was an accomplished woman, who taught beside the three Rs, music, wood-carving, a little natural history, and elementary history, geography and 'English'.

Three things Willie learnt of her that he never forgot: Browning's 'Pied Piper', Gray's 'Elegy', and Shelley's 'Skylark'. He shared his father's and grandfather's memory – for what he liked. And even at the age of eight he like these.

It may be remarked that they were, especially the two last, queer poems for a child's fancy, (one wonders also at the queer wisdom of the teacher as well) and there is no doubt that a full understanding of their beauties did not come till later. But an appreciation of the fuller beauties of art comes to grown-ups gradually too:– with repetition, and with pondering, and above all with the corroboration of life.

Life alone enforces such lines as these:–

'We look before and after,
And pine for what is not.
Our sincerest laughter
With some pain is fraught;
Our sweetest songs are those which tell of saddest thought.'

Willie without (as God forefend) this larger realisation, liked the verses; and because he liked them he learned them; and because he learned and liked, never forgot them.

He learned also to carve a bellows for his mother, and to know the names and habits of certain common trees, insects, and wild flowers. And he learned to sing. Perhaps it would be more accurate to say that he embraced an officially sanctioned opportunity of doing something that he had always enjoyed doing. Song is essentially a natural, and not an acquired attribute. It has its technique like any other art, but the fact remains plainly expressed by one of our greatest artists that:– 'The basis of all good singing is the desire to sing. Singing is, was, and always will be a joyous impulse. Without that, it may or may not be technique: it is not singing.

That impulse Willie possessed, and indulged to the full in 'Widdicombe Fair', 'John Peel', and 'Barbara Allen'. His passion for sweet and ordered sound dated at least as far back as petticoat days and before he could do more than – at the first phrase played – crawl along the passage to the room where the piano was. Also he was not alone in his pilgrimages, although Eric had not been born, and was in the words of his brother's later taunt 'only half a seed'.

You would probably not guess that Willie's companion then was a hedgehog. This queer little beast which inhabited the garden for one summer actually ran races with the boy in order to listen to the music. Do not think this a story invented – Why should it be? – it is not clever enough. It merely happened. Scores of times, on the player going to the door to open it, she (for it was usually Mrs. Harvey) found the baby and the prickly pig together on a mat.

The child sang, but the hedgehog didn't, through it screamed terribly and almost as loudly as a stuck pig when trodden on.

Besides the things already mentioned Willie greatly enjoyed two books that were read to them by Miss Bradley. One was called *Madam How and Lady Why* and the other *The Heroes*. They were both by the same writer.

The reading (in their lunch hour) took place usually under the old chestnut tree, which had a nice though lumpy natural seat in its toes. On this Miss Bradley sat while the boys lay in the grass at her feet listening, and playing with the fallen brown polished chestnuts, and their cases that seemed to Willie to resemble green hedgehogs. He learned then that the prickles served for the same purpose to both plant and animal in protecting the life inside. It was knowledge of this sort, dropped casually, that he grasped, and made his own, rather than that of the school-room.

There, in spite of his two years handicap, Eric mainly beat him. His was a quiet plodding nature; Willie's curious and erratic. Eric at that age learnt because he was told to do so, but curiosity, which impelled Willie to tie a worm in a know to see whether he could undo himself, was the only thing which caused him to learn. Once his curiosity was roused he could learn twice as fast as his brother, but till that was done he could, or would not learn at all.

A chart of Eric's progress would show a straight line slanting steadily upward. Willie's went rather in a series of irregular jags:– the upward shoots showing the exact points at which subjects had seized his imagination. In this sense, he had no will power.

Eric's will drove his brain like a little horse. Neither boy had the slightest aptitude for arithmetic, but Eric did his sums. Willie didn't. When he was kept in, he waited till Miss Bradley had turned her back, and then – escaped. He had none of the sense of duty which caused his small and breathless brother to chase one of the hens for three quarters of an hour on a hot afternoon, not out of playful cruelty, but because, if you please, he had heard someone remark that such a hen ought not to be allowed to sit.

Another of Eric's mysterious characteristics is illustrated in a stock phrase of frequent annoyance to Miss Bradley having been at pains to draw and contrast the characters of an historical period. The men were possibly King Henry 8th and Cardinal Wolsey. 'And were they good men?'

This, in a little piping treble, was always Eric's enquiry. And it drove Miss Bradley nearly wild. Sometimes Willie would join in the persecution. But this was merely to tease the poor thing. Eric was serious. He hated to think that they were not good men, however appearances might seem to be against them.

This is the more curious because his knowledge of good and evil was no greater than those ancestors of ours before they had fallen to the lure of the subtil serpent. Eric was so obviously still in Eden – a rosy-cheeked cherub dressed in a sailor suit!

'Were they good men?' 'Was he a good man?' The phrase in all its possible variations became a sort of proverb. It was a saying which endured as a humorous catch phrase between the brothers as long as they lived. Years after in trenches Willie heard the self-same guiltless enquiry uttered and was torn between tears and laughter.

They were two lucky boys not only in having a rather remarkable woman as their teacher, but also in that added freedom which resulted from her remaining also housekeeper upon her brother's farm. My previous reference to governesses carried no ill-intentioned meaning. These boys were lucky in being taught for two hours every day and in being not 'governed' during the rest of it. (It would certainly have been hard to find anyone capable of doing it.) They were lucky in that their attendance 'at school' caused them to walk each day through a mile of Gloucestershire meadows. (Here much is suppressed that could be uttered).

They were lucky most of all, in a fellowship which then first sprang up between them founded upon common duties (done or avoided) and cemented by the fights and wrestles which prolonged their ramble home so that Bill Trigg who watched them from a turnip-field on the hill averred that on more than one occasion a short half-mile took them the best part of two hours to journey.

These two boys could fairly fight, and then forget. They were only children.

CHAPTER II

'Shades of the prison house'

In shadow of the tower, joined actually to the Chapter House, and forming part of the structure of the great Cathedral of Gloucester is 'The King's School'.

Hither, soon after they had been promoted to knickerbockers, came Willie and Eric. Here they were taught the usual things.

But more important than what they were taught, were the things they learned. And these things were bound up less with their lessons than with the place.

It was one of the schools founded by King Henry the Eighth, no doubt from the spoil of the monasteries. Over its windows were lettered the names of famous Gloucestrians which included those of John Whitcliffe, and Robert Raikes, whose first Sunday School (suggested by the sight of so many wretchedly tattered and fighting ragamuffins in the Sunday streets of his own city), was located in a small half-timbered house near by.

Neither he, nor that other, the great preacher (to many chiefly famous as having lived at a Gloucester Inn mentioned by Fielding in *Tom Jones*), caused the boys much thought, but they could not help being influenced by the general atmosphere of the place they lived in, and especially by that of the city surrounding it.

Every Monday morning their mother drove them into town in the pony cart, dropping them a street or two from the school in tender anticipation of those tears which at first sprinkled that six-day parting. And each Saturday (which was market day) their father took them home in his gig.

This was a great day. After the mid-day meal, for which, being weekly boarders, they remained, they set out for the market through streets of a city crammed with country people.

Through crowds jostling but invariably courteous they drifted to the market square, tree-shadowed, divided into sections for accommodation of the beasts then to be sold. The horse sheds were on one side. By three o'clock the business of the day was often done, and the boys and their father would watch the unsold animals side-lined up, and started home, before driving out together in the gig.

But on important fair days and especially at Barton Fair much might be seen of humour and excitement ere the market closed.

Then hundreds of tiny Welsh ponies invaded the square; and scores of wild green-ribboned Irish horses shown off by yet wilder Irishmen who ran them up and down regardless of any life or limb till purchased – possibly for mere safety's sake – by one or other of the scramblers.

'Hurroo! oo! Look at him! Look at him, gintlemen! The rent payer! The fortune teller! What's his colour worth? What's his shoulders worth? Stands like a lion! Walks like a lawyer's clerk! Gallops like the host of hell! None of your yearlings with his tail done up! Look at his teeth. Oo! Hurroo!'

People were knocked down, but nobody ever hurt, so far as one could see. They just got up and bought the animal that did it! It was a great time for the boys who watched. And beside all this there was a pleasure fair of 'Roundy-Horses', 'Swinging-Boats', Cokernut-shies', with endless side-shows of 'Fat Women', 'Skeleton Man', and freaks generally.

They would not have been boys had they not liked the pleasure fair better, at the time, and begged for another round on the steam horses when they might have been riding a live one at the head of six others into the quiet country, or sitting behind their father's old mare in the gig watching the lamp-shine on the playing buckles till they turned the last corner round the rick-yard and were home.

The truth is that the things which most impressed them were not the things which influenced them most. The things which influenced them most, they took for granted. They were happening so regularly, so quietly, as not to be noticed.

Take them in order. First the pang of separation (though but for a week) from home, and with that pang which never lessened, (although its expression in babyish tears soon changed into cheery 'Good-byes'), a growing consciousness of what home meant to them, and an increasing value put upon that meaning.

Continued small shocks of parting caused a continual pondering over what was left behind, and an increasing fondness; for it is Life's rule that love shall so be begotten upon human hearts:– that is by separation: and also that the greater the love the greater the sense of separation. Saints to God, lovers to the beloved, children to their homes, the double paradox holds, and is that to know, one must be separated, and that the nearer one comes again the greater is the division seen to be. Spiritually considered what is all this earthly existence but a chance to know God by separation from Him. In the womb of His thought how could we, being unconscious, know Him, and how love? But once born ...

This Truth is (as the newspapers have it), applicable to all things to which Truth may be applied, but our concern is in its application to Willie and Eric.

The first and most enduring result then, of their becoming weekly boarders at the King's School was this love of home. It never left them.

The second was an experience which was to be widened all through life – contact with and criticism of quite unfamiliar people.

Criticism – whether appreciation or depreciation – demands standards. These, the boys had, in their father and mother and the farm hands:– kindly people. Kindness of men and of the earth was an atmosphere they were familiar with – the only one.

It was with a feeling of bewildered astonishment that they took breaths in an atmosphere which was undeniably different. Not that there was any bullying of the Tom Brown sort at this school; only they encountered beings so different from those to whom they had been accustomed.

One single incident may stand in illustration. On the first day, utterly un-self-conscious: with no shyness; Willie in the 'break' went with the rest of his class into a play-space (it was not a ground, but a gravelled walled-in space) where larger boys were kicking about a tennis ball.

'What's your name?' asked a big boy.

'Willie Harvey' he answered at once.

The big boy laughed. He took Willie's cap and flung it over the wall.

'What's your name?' he asked Eric, as Willie still gaped in astonishment; and without waiting for a reply, he took his cap, and flung it in the same direction.

Poetic justice being awake and observant sent to the aid of Willie seven insane devils who roused him from his trance and caused him suddenly and with violence to kick the tormentor's shin, and while he rubbed it, to seize and send his cap to join the other two. The bell rang. A master came up. Vengeance was postponed.

This is sufficient to indicate the beginning of a process of education for which little more can be said than that it fits boys for the world. Willie had 'stood up for himself' – and his brother. Never till then had it been necessary.

And a yet more interesting fact is that, with allowances for age, he and the cap-thrower became very good friends.

Another introduction to our age, and the world into which they were to pass at a later date, was through the masters, whom they found to be very different from Miss Bradley.

The difference was largely the same difference as exists between employers of labour in the old days and employers of labour to-day. It was absence of personal contact, and it was due not to the men themselves but to a system.

These shareholders in their limited company for an also limited education were kind people – as kind maybe as their former single employer – but the present system of business caused that kindness to remain at home. Their concern was to teach, and it had to do with pupils – not boys; in the same way as modern business concerns itself with 'hands' – not men.

The result was a rather similar antagonism which if unreasonable was not without excuse.

Neither of the boys had ever attempted to cheat Miss Bradley though they might on occasions defy her, but now …

Eric acquired his nickname Hezekiah through the audible whisper of that word in class to Willie. In home work and upon every other occasion possible Willie did Eric's essays, and Eric did Willie's sums. It was of any permanent value only that it cemented an already firm friendship. The system provided a common enemy to be fought and hoodwinked wherever possible:– needless to say that was not so often as they hoped, for masters are not all fools. But they only made them the more cunning.

Such was their common practice and in the circumstances it was inevitable. There are schools of size which still advertise a special and personal interest in their pupils. No doubt they do their best, and think that what they say is true, but it is a lie. The system makes such a thing impossible.

This is to generalise. But to come to facts, Eric once attempted to treat a sympathetic master as he would have treated Miss Bradley – as a friend. Trigg had found a mumruffin's next in a tall hedge at home and Eric possessed with excusable excitement communicated the news as soon as he came into class on Monday morning. But the lesson happened to be scripture. His friend promptly (and no doubt rightly) snubbed him and twenty four boys roared with laughter.

For this and similar reasons life for the two boys came to be lived, not in school where in an ideal society it would be lived most fully, but outside; and then, since they were young, not on playing fields, but rather at home, in the week-ends.

Long after Eric had forgotten or put away all the conventional mental equipment he donned at that academy of learning he remembered the mumruffin's nest pointed out by the finger of Bill Trigg.

A ball of feathers with a long tail, known to Gloucestershire folks as the mumruffin, is elsewhere called the long-tailed tit, or in certain country places 'Bottle Tom'. Its beautiful oval nest formed of wool and moss, coated with lichen and lined with feathers, is in every sense of that ill-used word a marvel.

In this snug cradle it will rear twelve or more young, and in winter months you may see the whole family flitting with undulating movements from tree to tree, and hanging in an inverted positions from the ends of small twigs in search of insect food.

Its nest that year was in an apple orchard opposite the farm house, and both boys were enthralled in watching the family's weekly progress. Even after Barton Fair, the first thing they did on arriving home was to rush out to the place to see that fruit pickers had not disregarded their emphatic orders that the little home was not to be interfered with.

And it had not been. The King's command would have been no more effective to those labourers (we do not call them 'hands' in the country) than the wishes of those two children.

But besides this love intensified by separation of their home and the country: besides the little world of new characters driving them to re-value the old: besides the spectacle of bustling life which so richly coloured the ancient city each market day: there still remains to reckon as a influence: quiet.

Teaching at the school shall not detain us further than to say that it aimed at grounding rather than grinding. The Oxford and Cambridge local examinations were essayed annually with fair but not overwhelming success; and 'honours', being rewarded with a school holiday, were eagerly hoped for even by those who had no ambition to attain them. But the passing of examinations was no worshipped fetish even among the masters. 'You come here not so much to learn, as to learn how to learn' was a favourite and salutory saying of the 'heads' at their annual giving of prizes.

The motto was admirable. Whether the means of enforcing it were as ideal may be questioned, but at least they were those generally accepted then that Bill Trigg was educated and some of the masters were not. Exactly.

As was to be expected from the ages of the boys, it was during this period that they successively made the discovery of their sex, without however any noticeable signs of that hysteria now fashionably attaching to puberty owing to the works of writers not uninfluenced by a popular taste for such things.

The discovery of a natural appetite is neither good nor bad; but it is not likely to be particularly 'refined', especially when the young voyager is directed by fellow school-mates.

That was, and is still the general though not invariable custom of schools. Obviously it is not a good one; although less productive of permanent harm than we are asked (against experience) to believe by certain sex-obsessed moderns.

The Church is in many ways a wise old mother.

The school was, as I have said, a cathedral school. Mother Church's old-fashioned physic for growing pains was annually administered to those boys who seemed to require it. Were not confirmation regarded as a sacrament it might still be regarded as a medicine. Of course it is both – the one through the other.

Willie and Eric, or to be more precise Harvey I and Harvey II, were both (but not in the same year) confirmed at the cathedral in shadow of which they worked and played: whose choristers were their school-fellows: whose chimes twice by day and night for those four years flung a single quaint tune upon the wind.

Consider without foolish flippancy or hysterical exaggeration that physical change which had come upon them, and its more than physical potencies. Comprehend, if only from this natural standpoint, the gathering up and turning of this tidal force into channels of spiritual ardour and brave adventure.

Attach these happenings by association to an image of steadfast beauty, visible, tangible, familiar almost as home: an historical monument, a marvel of architectural achievement, and aspiration: a house of worship for a thousand years!

Having done this you will realise the influence at a certain point and thereafter exercised on the lives of two small boys by Gloucester Cathedral.

CHAPTER III

'The midnight roar
Of waves upon the shore
Of Rossall dear:
And on the pane,
The gusty rain
He loved to hear.'

You are tired of being ordered about. When is something going to happen? You want the story, Now, now, gentle reader! Like many other people you want something for nothing. What you call the story is easily written, and I am as impatient as you: - but we must earn it, if it is to be of any true pleasure or use to us.

In covering fourteen important years in seven chapters I have already restricted my output to the amount insisted upon by the Amalgamated Federation of British Readers; but every house must have a foundation – even the airy castle of the novelist – and I am not going to let men fall down by avoidance of a little healthy sweat good for us both. If what you want is a fool's paradise, you can find it elsewhere. I am going to build.

In this building of mine, the land makes the characters: the characters make the plot: and the land, characters, and plot, make the story.

Very well then, Willie left the King's School soon after he was fourteen, and went to Rossall. Eric remained on for two more years, and was confirmed in the Cathedral as already stated.

It was the first time that the brothers had been separated, and the result is important as an influence upon their relations similar to that which has been shown to have happened on the occasion of their leaving home.

At a time when each was developing his own individual tastes and character, this separation broken by holiday meetings enabled them to stand off from one another and so cement affection with critical understanding.

Rossall was a school of some three hundred boys, standing upon the bleak north west coast of England, in Lancashire.

As was to be expected, Willie found it a place very different from the one he had left.

It was self-contained – making even its own gas – and absolutely isolated from the world. Leave to visit either of the towns – that is Fleetwood (which was three miles off) or Blackpool (which was about six) was granted at half term on special application by visiting parents. Save for this, or breaking bounds, you did not quit the school grounds from the moment you stepped inside at the beginning of term to the time of 'breaking up'.

In the absence of a single outside interest, the boys threw themselves wholeheartedly into those of the school, or perished of boredom.

Like all our great public schools it was a monastic institution administered on the monitorial system, and it provided a fine Spartan training. Work and games were compulsory – especially the latter.

It was not a very pleasant existence for a 'mens' however 'sana' otherwise than 'in corpore sano'. But for any undiluted slacker it was hell.

Willie was fortunate. His old grandfather would have turned in his grave to see that vitality of his put to such uses as Willie put it upon the football field; on the shore at hockey; and at cover point during haymaking time.

On arrival he found himself in one of the eight houses – and of course the best. After a short period of homesickness, and disgusted marvelling at the extreme ugliness of the country around, he threw himself heart and soul into games, and succeeded.

At work he was fortunate again in acquiring easily, and indeed without consciously aiming for it, the most useful of all class reputations. He was looked upon as a painstaking fool.

This to an extent he deserved, since he did at times really try; and the beneficent result was that before long he was enabled occasionally to devote himself to what he liked – which was a good thing – without paying any heavy penalty in lines and other impositions – which are bad things.

The truth is that while his body fitted excellently into 'the system', his mind did not.

Thus in English literature he would not have been out of his class in the sixth form where he would have taken some interest in it.

In Mathematics he was out of his class even in Form I.

Form VI would have encouraged his interest in History and Geography to learn which he needed only to have been shown the interdependence of these subjects and their influence on modern life. Drawing he would never have learned, having no aptitude.

Form I fitted him for modern languages, which he had not till then attempted. In Scripture he would have fluctuated between and top and bottom of the school. He could never learn the lists of kings of Israel and Judah, though he had an uncanny knowledge of the Book of Job, much of which he knew by heart. He really cared for the gospels, that is for the story of Christ, and His teaching, and was fascinated by parts of Revelation. The rest he ignored save for the rhythm of certain splendid phrases which stuck in his memory.

As for Music, he would not practise his scales, but won the school singing competition as a dark horse. Also he came out third in the school on a general knowledge paper at the age of fifteen – his class being Form IV. Well, what are you to do with a boy like that? 'The system' demands that the test of your chain of learning shall be its weakest link. You cannot blame its priests for putting such an one in a class fitting his ignorance. You can hardly blame the victim for thinking life in school hours dull when even the things he liked were made babyish and of no significance to the mind. You can readily excuse his form masters in such an atmosphere of distortion for regarding him kindly as a nice dull boy to be excused for his keenness on the cricket field.

Had his parents known the true state of affairs they would undoubtedly have considered their money wasted. But in fact it was not wasted, but spent for things other than they knew.

Willie's three years at Rossall were of very real value. If he learned little, at least he escaped cramming his head with a lot that was no use to him ... When his position in the house (acquired solely through games) could no longer be ignored he was made a monitor. As such he gradually acquired tact, learned to shoulder responsibility, to take quick decisions, and to appreciate and use organisation.

Almost all the good he got out of Rossall derived from his House rather than his School. There he was an influence. In addition to his power in directing the tendencies of elder boys, he acquired a great popularity with the smaller and unimportant members of the house. By immemorial custom they should have been ignored. But nobody had suffered more from homesickness in early days than he, and a shamefaced tenderness to his successors in suffering showed that he remembered it. Many an apparently casual word of his dropped deep into the hearts of youngsters who in after days of power and security passed it on to make another link in the chain. It was like a handshake in hell. For of all agonies there is (I aver) none at once so bitter and so unfair as homesickness. Remorse for sin may be terrible, but at least it is fair. Homesickness is a harsh punishment of the gods visited upon all that is noble in man. It is virtue rewarded. It is an answer to all who expect ease as a reward of righteousness and not rather a noble discomfort.

The unconventional kindness of Harvey was untouched by any such philosophic musings. He did these things, as he did most other things; because he couldn't help himself. The halo of a moral reformer he must also lack, since the House was in a clean and strenuous period, and not one scandal occurred in it during his three years. He never even coveted that halo.

One night soon after he had been made a monitor he lay listening to rain. It was drumming a fitful music upon the window of his cubicle. The wind clamoured for admittance, singing wild sea shanties and then (softly) scraps of some lonely tune from Ireland. As the wind's voice rose and fell so the rain varied it accompaniment. It drummed lustily during the loud sea choruses. It was like old sailors thumping fists upon a table beating tipsy time. When the voice sank down to a dreamy lullaby, that drumming softened to the slightest sibilant little sleepy tapping conceivable. It was like soft little kisses through the song of a mother crooning to her baby. Dream kisses of dream children; fluttering of little wings upon the darkened panes. Through all this the persistent pulse of the Sea, now harsh now muted came incessantly in a rhythmic undertone.

Willie sat up in bed listening. It was the sweetest moment of the day. His cubicle was on one side of the dormitory he controlled. The window faced the sea. He put his face to the cold panes and gazed into the darkness. The moods of the wind and rain had got into his head a haunting tune called 'Spanish Ladies', and then, overlapping that, the memory of his mother: home: his sweet child's life to be lived never more except in such hours. The dormitory was silent save for the heavy breathing of sleepers. The school clock struck one: a single not which was instantly swallowed up in the soft noises of the night.

Suddenly the salt-crusted music: the sweet heartache, were dispelled with an unfamiliar sound. The old curiosity awoke. He listened intently, and heard, first, faint footsteps; then the noise of a lower window being carefully opened; and next a rustling sound of entrance followed by a thud as somebody jumped from the sill into a study below. A burglar perhaps, but more likely a boy... Anyway, Willie was not one to wake up others to share the excitement of a capture. He slipped out of bed, and fled barefooted along the passage and downstairs where he waited concealed in a doorway.

A soft shuffling ... Someone treading nervously in stockinged feet ... A moving shadow darker than the rest ... Willie sprang out, and brought it down upon the tiling with a clatter of boots carried in hands.

The prisoner, after fighting furiously, lay still – a knee on each biceps: then gasped, 'You're choking me!' Willie's hands relaxed a little on his throat.

'Who are you?'

'Bowman.'

'What!' Bowman was their outside left. 'And the House match against Christie's to-morrow:– You swine!'

'I haven't been – '

'What do I care where you've been, or what you've done – damn you! No wonder you played the stinking game you did last Satur ... Lord, here's "Chow"!' 'Chow' was the housemaster. His heavy unmistakeable steps were heard on the upper landing.

'Oh God! What shall I do? I'll be sacked. My mother ... Help me out of it, Harvey ... O God!'

Willie pushed him into a study.

'You blasted fool!' he said.

A lighted candle appeared at the top of the stairs. It threw into relief a large ruddy face, and an iron grey moustache.

It descended flickering in little jerks. 'Who is there?' said a deep voice.

They Harvey clad in his pink pyjamas moved slowly from where he stood at the study door, and as if feeling his way, stepped steadily but blindly forward till he came into the vague circle of candlelight at the foot of the stairs.

'Harvey, what are you doing here?' asked the master sternly.

Without replying, the figure advanced with arms outstretched.

'Harvey!'

The boy paused; then continued his strange walk till he had actually singed his hair in the flame. 'Hands!' he suddenly cried. 'Hands there!'

The master looked at him curiously: then – put his arm round his shoulder, and guided him up the stairs and into his dormitory. When he had got the boy back into bed, he shook him awake.

'Harvey', he said, 'you've been sleep-walking.'

'What! What sir?' cried Harvey.

'Sleep-walking' repeated 'Chow'.

'Sleep-walking!' echoed Willie: then 'Sorry, sir!' 'Thought I was playing a house match' he added.

'Hm! you're thinking too much of football' remarked 'Chow', perhaps truely. 'Goodnight', and then, as he turned to leave the cubicle, 'Good luck for to-morrow, Harvey,' he said.

'Thank you, sir.'

Whether 'Chow' had guessed, or was actually deceived, Willie never decided. But they won the match. And Bowman never broke out again.

CHAPTER IV

'Look at the clock!'

Willie was leaving Rossall crowned (athletically speaking) with two school caps, robed in triple house colours, at the time when Eric was climbing steadily to a similar position in another school.

This school, which was smaller than Rossall, stood on the banks of the Thames within a few miles of Oxford. It had a long tradition, and was in many ways a larger and more lively edition of the King's School which he left soon after his confirmation.

Eric and the majority of the scholars were boarders, but there was a sprinkling of day boys, and there were no 'houses'. The school itself therefore circumscribed his life, and was to his activities what 'Chow' had been to Willie.

The development of Eric as a school character inevitably followed the lines of Willie's. His success was achieved through games, and by dint of something else. You may call it character.

At this time, and from this time on, the difference in the two boys was very marked. Eric was then stretching into a tall loose-limbed lad whose chief physical attribute, whether shown in those sweet effortless off-drives past cover on a cricket field, or on the football field in his swerving yet straight run at centre forward, was grace: Willie hardening into the stocky strength and ungainly swiftness evident in his play at outside right, and that hawklike pounce upon the swerving cricket ball at extra cover. (A hard drive between cover and 'extra' almost invariably swerves from right to left of the fieldsman.)

And if their physical differences were great, their mental and spiritual differences were (as may be guessed from preceding history) not less.

Yet it is a fact that the chief difference between them was cause of the chief similarity:– that already mentioned success in games, particularly in such games as demand and almost detached steadiness of nerve in the player.

While both were admirably, though differently, equipped in body for such success, it must be allowed that many others, less successful, were equipped equally well, if not better. Many were as lithe and graceful as Eric: as strong as Willie. Also it must be admitted that the remarkable vitality of their grandfather found parallel in that of a number of boys descended through other genealogy.

The important distinction was another matter rooted rather in a certain unconscious preoccupation – in Willie's case with a mysterious Something described already (though undefined) in that chapter wherein he is shown as having glimpsed a certain secret beauty of Earth: and in Eric's case, with another Something perhaps more consciously defined, equally deep-rooted:– the thought of God.

The foolish may laugh at such an explanation, but the fact remains that each by reason of his persistent, unconscious, preoccupation, wad enabled to rise to 'occasions' with a lack of 'nerves' astounding to their fellow players. And this was due directly to the fact that although consciously and upon the surface each was as anxious to win – to do justice to the side – as any boy in the team, there was already in each Something, huge, not to be ignored even though forgotten, to assure them that the 'occasion' was not so great as it seemed: which made each of them treat any match as an ordinary match, with appreciable benefit in the result.

It could hardly be said of either that he had found vocation. Only he had achieved a beneficent indifference to all that was not vocation. The whisper which said 'This is not the occasion' was already audible. The trumpet proclaiming 'The great occasion is now!' was not, as yet. This is to repeat that in work and in games a similar preoccupation posessed the boys, which sometimes assisted them in a trial of nerves. And this is to foreshadow the whole future of their story.

But soon enough will each follow his own thorny maze in quest of Something! Soon enough the vague and wavering shapes of Vocation will take substance crying to them over star-crowned mountains and rivers deep as Death! Soon, soon, the strenuous quiet dream of school-days shatter upon the wilder dream of adolescence!

Let us forbear awhile to observe or consider the steady growth of the tree of knowledge, even though its fruit be for the healing of the nations, and not as that other. Eden awaits us yet for a little while; and, since all things come to their close, we are fools to anticipate expulsion.

See then, the Thames meadows golden-green in summer light. See a cluster of school buildings in blue June air. See eleven flannelled boys wearing caps of cherry and white; a host of others lounging round or lying in small companies on the grass to watch the season's most important match while devouring cherries from paper bags. A sprinkling of old boys and elder brothers are present. The school is batting.

A fast bowler wearing a blaring Zingari cap has, perhaps by means of its disturbing visual and moral effect, perhaps by reason of a slightly short-length ball with a capacity for 'flying', taken or caused other to take, five good school wickets at a total cost of forty runs.

The school clock strikes five from its high tower above the bowling scrum at one end of the ground. There is an hour left for play. One hundred and two runs are required for victory, but the school have already given up expecting that. Even a draw is too good to hope for.

'Harvey is the only one who isn't frightened of that brute in the cap' remarked one youthful disgusted critic to another. But that was not true. The wickets had been lost not by funking, but by foolishness, which caused them to feel timidly forward at bowling, which they over-rated, usually with the result of a slip-catch, followed by a deeply-reflective walk back to the pavilion.

Out of the total of forth, Harvey had made twenty-three simply by stepping out and driving the good length balls, and leaving the short ones alone in the manner they had all been taught.

'Harvey is a good bat, but one good bat can't save us now'; commented the youthful disgusted critic's next neighbour. 'Oh, good shot!' It was a lovely off-drive, but the out field sprinting along the boundary turned the four into three, and the net ball saw Harvey's partner edge a ball from the fast bowler into the hands of first slip. Six for forty three.

Then emerged from the pavilion a white-faced boy with set mouth – Hawkins II, who was being played for the first time in a school match, chiefly on account of a big amaze in form games in which nobody seemed able to bowl him out. He was the last 'bat' on the side; the others being a magnificent wicket-keeper, played solely for that reason, and two bowlers whose amaze as such exceeded by almost as much again their amaze as run-makers.

Eric, who had come down the pitch to meet him, whispered something into his ear, and left him to face the last ball of 'Cap's' over.

What that whispered something was, may be guessed by the fact that the next ball – a short bumping delivery on the off, was allowed to pass without any semblance of a stroke being made by Hawkins minor, whose bat remained rooted in the block-hole.

Off the next over Eric scored sixteen, and then secured 'Cap's' bowling by calling Hawkins for a run off a stroke which pushed the ball no more than six yards from the pitch. With his partner backing up it was an easy single, although it occasioned vociferous warning and advice from the spectators.

He played five balls of the next over; the first and third being driven for fours; the two between being left severely alone, and the fifth hooked off his eyebrows for three. Hawkins II stopped the last.

Then the bowling was changed, and Eric was missed in the long field of the second fall amid audible gasps. But the over yielded nine runs, and the score now stood at eighty, of which his own contribution was precisely sixty three.

the complexion of the game was not completely altered. Enthusiasm was roused in the spectators, who saw if not victory in sight at least the prospect of a good finish made possible by an exhibition of fearless hitting such as had not been seen that season.

Eric got a four and a three off the fast bowler, and Hawkins got a knock on the jaw, but he played out the over, and more than earned a clap on the back from his partner.

The opposing captain changed his tactics. Seven men were put on the leg side, and a slow good length bowler put on with the object of getting Eric caught. But with rather more than half an hour to go, and but sixteen runs now wanted, that batsman was taking no risks.

Four overs yielded as many runs, of which one was a leg-bye for Hawkins, who was using his pads quite as frequently as his bat.

The duel between bowler and batsman which had developed, though far less spectacular than the previous big hitting had been, was if anything even more exciting. Each stroke was followed keenly by the spectators, and a round of applause rewarded every run made or saved.

The other bowler, using the left-hander's natural break away, kept a fine length, bowling rather wide, with his men on the off.

Thus at five minutes to six the two boys were still together, and eight runs were wanted. And then indeed the eyes of all the school wandered between the wickets and the school clock, whose six silvery strokes were by tradition immemorial the signal for drawing stumps. For it was Hawkins and not Eric who faced the bowler.

He had been playing like a brick wall; but a brick wall does not make runs, and it was felt that the game depended on the last over of the day, which would in the almost certain absence of scoring be bowled by the leg-break bowler to Eric.

This proved the truth. But no one present guessed, or could have been expected to guess, the fashion in which that memorable match was to be decided.

When Eric, jumping out of his crease a couple of yards, took the slow bowler's first delivery full pitch, and with a mighty hit lifted it high over the bowler's screen, and banged the face of the school clock, everyone became almost delirious with joyous excitement. A sixer! Golly, what a sixer! That leaves two runs for a win (only one for a draw!), and five balls to get 'em off! And Harvey …

But what's this? The umpire is making signs. The batsmen cross over. By the Lord, the umpire is right too! That straight drive was a short boundary from the place where the pitch was made for the Old Boys' match, and it was agreed beforehand that 'three to', and 'five over', should be the scores. Clearly, the particular hit in question would if run out result in about seven runs, but that may nor affect the decision. The old boys are willing to concede the six runs. Neither of the batsmen is quixotic enough to refuse to take them in the circumstances. Mere justice is all in favour of acceptance. But five was agreed on. The umpire has signalled five. Five it is. Go on!

In an oppressive silence the two boys cross over. One minute remains for play. So soon as strikes six o'clock stumps will be drawn. That is a tradition no more to be disobeyed than an umpire's. Why? It was a rule before ever cricket was invented. Generations of dead scholars had ceased their play at that hour asking the same question – Why? Even then nobody knew. How typical of England!

'Now go for 'em', advises Eric. There is no need to whisper that advice. It is patent. Hawkins II lashes out at the first ball and misses it. He lashes out at the second, and is bowled. Before he has reached the pavilion, his successor (the wicket keeper) is taking a hasty centre. Bang! He is out also. Two players are on their way to the pavilion together, and a third rushing madly to the wickets wearing but a single pad! He faces the bowler. He leaps out; yorks himself with a half volley; and the bowler has done the hat-trick!

There is yet one ball to go. That ball is smitten at, and missed by the next batsman – if such title can by courtesy be his. But is also misses the wickets. 'Over'!

Eric had meanwhile been looking at the clock. 'You didn't call 'last over' did you?' he asked the umpire. "Course not', replied that worthy, 'we plays till the clock strikes, as you knows, Mr Harvey.' 'Well then, John', said Eric, as he commenced to roar with laughter, 'Well then, look at it, John. Loo-loo-look! It's stopped!'

'An' no wonder,' answered the groundsman, 'ater that punch you giv' 'im. And I've knowed 'e wer' stopped, Mr Harvey, for the last five balls, I 'ave, and don't you forget it zur.'

Like a bush fire, the joke spread. Players, and onlookers alike wallowed in its deliciousness. And after they had picked themselves up, the lefthanded bowler began another over with the tears still streaming down his cheeks.

And Eric straightaway hit him to the screen – the other one – and won the match.

PART III

VOCATION

CHAPTER I

'Belief in plan of Thee enclosed in Time and Space
Health, peace, salvation universal.'

A man who has found his vocation is happy. A man who has none, is contented. Sheer misery is reserved for those who have vocations, but have not discovered them.

For this reason the unhappiest period in the lives of a great majority of people is that which they must live immediately after leaving school. For it is the one damning criticism to be levelled indiscriminately against schools, whether public, private, board, or whatever other kind can be thought of and mentioned, that they do not aim at the discovery of vocation, but rather at pushing of boys through a net the meshes of which are all of one size.

Why (It is a stage through which we may pass swiftly, hopping the years in pursuit of but one thing – the tale) – still why, you may ask, was Willie made a solicitor, and Eric put into a bank?

Simply for the reason that you, reader, were made an engineer, a grocer, or an accountant. Willie was good at English. He could express himself. Eric's reports praised his mathematics. He could manage figures.

Both boys were asked what they would like to be. No doubt you too, gentle reader, were asked. But did you know? Possibly you developed early, and did know. These two boys did not. Willie indeed agreed that a passionate appeal for lost causes would be acceptable to his temperament. He thought (quite wrongly of course) that a solicitor's life would be concerned with such, rather than with the prosaic transfer of property at profit from one man to another. Eric, wanting only to be a good man, was willing to be whatever his parents liked.

But what, save reports, had they to guide them? – poor dears! They had, at some sacrifice, given the boys 'a good education'; but that meant that for ten years, in which they might have been finding out, they had save for holidays, been separated from their children. What could they do, but follow the school report?

For two years prior to the events of the last chapter Willie had ridden in to St. John's Chambers, on Marigold his mare (a daughter of Buttercup) to be initiated as an articled clerk into the law and its practice. During that time he passed the preliminary and intermediate examinations of the Law Society, and kept a diary.

It is not an account of his struggles to pass these examinations, but an extract from the diary – the extract which in fact concludes it – which seems best worth incorporating into this story.

September 12th, 1907. – 'Death is inexorable. Man and beast sullenly await the cold of its coming. But Life is – what? …

Since I started reading for "The Final" I have not attended Chambers except for mornings. Afternoons are devoted to book-work. In fine weather I have been accustomed to use "the old ruins" (to-day part of a cattle shed) where tradition has it that black Dominicans pursued similar study years past.

The place is fresh-aired, and a convenient shelter from the wind that likes to turn over pages before one is ready: also a retreat from those who delight in calling one to meals at inopportune moments.

Yesterday at the usual time I had settled myself to read beneath the great paneless window through which admittance is given at an angle to the afternoon sunshine, when my attention following intermittently the progress of light across the floor was taken by a sudden glimmer of unexpected colour. It lay at the foot of a sun beam – round and greenish.

My curiosity was roused to make an examination. I discovered an old very worn copper ring lying in a groove. Recent rains had washed away the covering of soil. It gleamed back curiously from the grey stone. I took hold of it and gave it a strong pull. The slab remained steady. Again I tugged, so that the metal stretched and twisted in my hand. The ring wouldn't stand the stone's weight. Then suddenly it occurred to me that perhaps it was never intended to, and I pulled sideways. Instantly the block stirred; and at my second more determined tug, slid back into the wall revealing a flight of steps.

Striking a match, I descended, and found myself in a tunnel about four and a half feet high.

It was a tiny evil-smelling place with damp walls and slime-coated floor. The direction was apparently downward.

I crawled slowly along, as the roof became gradually lower. Presently the passage ended abruptly; possibly the walls had fallen in.

I lighted my last match and turned with some relief to find the way out. It was a cold, unromantic sort of place. I felt sorry I had come. Approaching my starting point, I suddenly noticed that no light was entering. At the foot of the steps when I arrived there was foul darkness. By some mysterious agency the stone had regained its place.

My hands slipped from the clammy surface as I tried with feverish haste to force aside the firm unyielding barrier of stone. Then, like a stab, the horrible truth came upon me:– I was buried – buried alive.

At that thought a sharp cry escaped me, and there seemed, for a moment, nothing to breathe. Then I regained control of myself. I shouted for a time at the darkness of the closed slab, but ceased to do so on reflecting how seldom the ruins were visited now that the outer wall had been pushed down by cattle, and was no more a keep for them.

I sat down on one of the steps, and thought:– "I must get out. I must get out." After that I set off exploring again on my hands and knees.

'There must be some way out', I kept repeating. It seemed so impossible that I should have to die. But ten minutes ago I had dozed in the sun and read a book named *Snell's Equity*, amused at the quaint and ancient phrase which described 'donatio mortis causa' as the gift of one "apprehending his dissolution near". Apprehending his dissolution near!

I crawled hurriedly along the floor of my filthy prison. Again the oozing walls closed in; the roof bent down: again I reached the end. It was the end also of my unreasonable hope. I knew now that I must die. No use whining, but oh, bitter so to perish, shut away from friends and the face of day! Though he may not know it, life is very sweet to a young man. I found that out.

"Well", thought I, "let me die as near sunshine as I can!" I started to crawl back to the steps. Blindly: feeling that narrow walls, I went. And then suddenly my right hand was stretching into emptiness ...

How I had missed this turning I don't know. Trembling I turned along the tiny passage. Till then, since the first shock of discovery, I had been calm. Now my breath started to come in strange sobs. Deliverance was in the pin-point of yellow light before me. I scrambled frenziedly forward; and reached the same steps down which I had descended. The slab had of course not stirred; but losing myself in a branch of the tunnel I had discovered that second, shut slab at the top of similar steps and mistaken it for the first – not unreasonably.

Such explanations came upon me as I pushed through into daylight. I thought them funny and I laughed aloud. Then I burst out crying. Why, I don't know. I had been self-possessed enough when faced with the prospect of death. But this was life. It was life that affected me so.

Ten minutes (that was all it was) had shewn me what it was to live.

I had never known before.

I staggered up into a new world.

What did it all mean?

– The wind?

– The sniff of the firs?

– The bare architectural beauty of elms?

It seemed that I was never less hysterical in my life. I was merely awake – for the first time.

It seemed a perfectly natural thing for me to roll dog-like among the leaves, and shatter with sobs the peaceful country silence.

I had left the ruins and was wandering through thin woods. I heard the ash saplings fighting together like men with quarter-staves. I heard, like sea-surf, the breeze in high beeches. Oh, the curious shadows!

A gong sounded faintly from the farm below me. It rumoured white bread, and yellow country butter, and honey as sweet and golden as the lamp-lit evening and evenings to follow.

My sobbing continued. I was not ashamed of it. It was a young fool's solemn thanksgiving for life – a young fool, but not a dead fool!

Still, I felt that I could not go home in such a state. It would frighten them. Besides I had forgotten my book ...

September 13th. This is Mother's birthday. I gave her Whitman's *Leaves of Grass*. It is a queer book especially in parts, but she understands life and me well enough to like it.

He speaks (It is as though he knew Minsterworth) of, "The blossoms, fruits of ages, orchards divine and certain, Forms, objects, growths, to spiritual images ripening."

And he goes on:–

"In Thy ensemble, whatever else withheld, withhold not from us Belief in plan of Thee enclosed in Time and Space, Health, peace, salvation universal."

74

I have always believed (quite how, and why, I do not know) that there is a spirit in things and in beasts as well as in men:– that matter really exists only to reveal the spiritual.

Revelation supports this belief with its account of cities, and gems, and trees which bear fruit under the natural law: and the disciples recognised Christ after he had risen. Minsterworth and those Malvern Hills and old Buttercup there, will in all that endears them to me be hereafter what they are now, because our souls are eternal, and whatever fits our souls is eternal also.

Since yesterday, which I count in some real way as my own birthday, (though that is truly in March) the following Whitman lines have greatly appealed to me:–

"Beginning my studies, the first step pleased me so:–
The mere fact consciousness, these forms, the power of motion,
I have hardly gone, and hardly wished to go further."

Trigg and I took lights and explored the mysterious passages beneath "The Old Ruin". He had "heard tell on 'em before", but never seen them.

Now they are to be filled in, as dangerous. Well, they have done their work …'

CHAPTER II

'Follow the gleam!'

Such was the beginning of Willie's consciousness of vocation, real, though undefined in expression.

He knew, in short, what he was to do, without knowing how he was to do it.

To the same stage, and to the same state of questioning and unhappiness came Eric, though by other roads.

What we have so far followed may be dealt with very shortly in retrospect. Here are two brothers of typically English breeding growing up and forming characters in an atmosphere of home and the public school. Temperamentally very different, they have grown to be firm friends, united by a single stream of inherited energy, turned into individual channels.

The course of those channels is the concern of this tale in its immediate future, but it may now be openly said without fear of such anticipation of the story as will result in anti-climax, how the energy referred to is in each manifesting itself. In Willie it is growing into a determination to produce art which will embody his now clear perception of the divine in common existence, lived as it should be – that is naturally. In Eric it is becoming in obsession of religious conviction. To the one, from henceforth, God's world must be everything: to the other, Christ's empire. This, if either is to achieve the fruit of his being.

The mode of Eric's discovery was less sudden and less dramatic than Willie's. And it is here that a grave artistic difficulty arises; for while no one doubts that a continuous dropping will wear away the stone, yet such does not constitute narrative from the reader's standpoint. For which reason I have divulged the end before the means; telling you of Eric's great ambition and forbearing to trace its growth, and the steps by which it achieved entire consciousness in his mind.

Let it suffice that work in a bank gradually but surely led him to a knowledge of his destiny, which was the taking of orders.

The period of doubt and questioning we can also pass over for sake of the story. I will tell you as shortly as possible what he did, so soon as he knew.

After the work of the day was done he sat up every night learning Greek, and he made arrangements for mortgaging his inheritance to an amount necessary to carry him through a necessary university training:– that is, he mortgaged his inheritance to the last penny. That was necessary.

Had he known what his future work would be, or had his masters divined it, the steady effectual industry of his school-days might have obtained him a scholarship to Oxford, and he been saved the later anxiety and labour of presenting himself years after as a commoner. At all events he would have learned Greek.

But he had not at that time discovered his vocation, and of course nobody did it for him: so the fact stands that he must be penalised in order to follow his only happiness:– that is his best use in the world.

The case is not uncommon: - almost I had said it was general! The difference is that few sufficiently 'believe' to start again. That is where Eric was different from others. Just so soon as he 'knew', he started afresh. And characteristically he did so patiently: a step at a time.

As well as any that could be imagined these two boys illustrated two separate sorts of courage, namely, daring and endurance. It is hard to say which is the more admirable, but there is no doubt as to which it is happier to possess. It is the old argument between a sprinter and a long distance runner. Each will excel in his event. But take life as it is, and it is the difference between the plodding, and the restive horse fastened to a plough. Each will work hard, but the one will fret himself to pieces with his plunging, while the other advances calmly in the furrow.

Both boys in their separate fashions had 'enlisted under the banner of the Holy Ghost', but while Eric retained always a patience with his drill sergeant, Willie's only cry was for 'bloody war and promotion'.

Both boys worked their hardest to attain proficiency. The difference (to be hereafter illustrated) was that Eric could wait, but Willie could never – at any rate with any peace of mind.

And one other point told also in favour of the younger brother and aided him in that patient persistency of his. He saw clearly the end of his furrow. Willie did not.

To be a clergyman, was, however strange to a family essentially yeoman, at least intelligible as an ideal. To be a poet (was it a poet Willie wanted to be?) was nothing of the sort. The way was wrapped everywhere in dense and drifting fog which showed even in its clearances a road leading nowhere.

Artists have almost invariably come from the middle classes, generally from yeoman stock, but this act of faith has always to be performed on the part of those who dare the calling, and through an even greater effort, by those loving them and concerned with their welfare.

To work oneself to tatters and be thought a waster (at times even by oneself) is the lot of every young artist, and it is not conducive to calm sustained effort. Eric could go to Oxford. There is no university of the arts. There is no encouragement:– only impenetrable mists of doubt and perplexity, bare bleak rocks of disappointment, and the companion mocking of all safe sensible people, whose feet tread not such outlandish and dangerous paths.

Yet one most common and bitter grief Willie at least escaped though only through a sorrow almost as keen. Before that spiritual warfare had resulted in open victory for the forces of apparent folly, his father died. He was so spared (as how many have not been spared!) the horrible pain of having to hurt one whom he loved and respected, and who loved him.'

His mother, both because she was a very remarkable woman, and because she was – his mother, would in time accept the nature of the son she bore.

His father, gentle and kind as he was, would never have done this. He would need to be broken and re-born and bred before he could understand.

It was enough disappointment that both his sons could have been lost to farming. In putting them to two respected professions he had gone to his utmost limit. His love and care he would certainly never have denied them – nor his purse. But to know that one of his sons had gone mooning, scribbling – mad ... This knowledge would only have filled him with the pity he gave to lunatics, and such as committed suicide. His poor son! ...

What would have happened to their grandfather, it is funny to contemplate. He would probably have burst!

Two good reasons prevented Willie from ever mentioning to his father this strange tendency towards literature and away from law.

The first was that he himself was but half converted to it till after his father's death. The second was a knowledge of the opposition it would provoke, and on top of this a stubborn instinct of chivalry, reverence, tenderness, or – something, which forewarned that we could not use what arguments he had for support of it, not because they would be ineffective as such, but because his ability to make use of them was the gift of a father who had worn himself with work to provide his sons with a good education. They would never intellectually convince him. They would only wound his feelings through his intellect. To do this was, it seemed to Willie, worse than taking a gift, and mocking the giver. He felt bad enough in breaking the news to his mother who could half way to meet him. No, he could not do it.

Keen as was the pang of that parting coming when it did, it was mercifully disposed (since the clash was bound to come) and a sense of this was at long last the most soothing balm to Willie's sorrow. Another was that the sensitive highly-strung nature of his beloved had been spared any long illness and lingering pain.

It befell one Saturday night. Both boys were home. They had assisted the village team in a football match, and returned elated with victory. Their father, who complained of pain in one of his legs, had gone to bed. His sons went into the bedroom and sat down on the ottoman to chat to him. He found pleasure in listening, and congratulated them on the result of their game.

Less than two hours later (about midnight) their mother woke them. They saw at once that she was frightened.

'Go, one of you, for the doctor at once' she said. 'Father is ill!' 'I'm afraid', she added sobbing, 'it is too late already.'

She was right. The clot of blood which had formed in a vein causing uneasiness in his leg, was not dislodged by hot fomentation and had been carried into the great heart valve. Already he was choking to death.

Marigold galloped that night as she had not galloped for many a year, and did never again. But her master was dead when the doctor arrived, to utter the single professional word – 'thrombosis!'

Neither of Mrs. Harvey's sons had seen death before, and it horrified them. In spite of the last majesty and imperturbable peace of the face after the features had been composed, and the jaw bound up, Willie never forgot a picture which he had glimpsed for a moment before riding away:– which had made him desperate in urging on the game old mare in her mad career.

Eric sat by it for an hour. What he thought, nobody could tell. He just prayed, and comforted his mother. But Willie was filled with a wild and questioning anger against heaven and earth and the God that governed them.

'Did You see that?' he shouted to the sky as he galloped. He lashed at the mare with his whip, and she nearly unseated him in her plunge. 'Did you see that? Did you allow that?' he cried savagely to God.

'That', was later to become a common sight in his eyes. 'That', was a manly flesh turned to ashes, brightness of eyes to an idiot stare, beauty to something at once hideous and comic, and this was the sting. Comic ...

The devil perhaps was amused. And God, what about Him? 'Hold up, damn you!' he shouted to the mare; and realising consecutively that it was his own careless riding that had caused her to stumble, he concentrated once more upon the work in hand:– to bring the doctor.

Severn here wound in a loop of river which the road followed per-force since there was no bridge. Two miles and more would be saved if he could go direct. But how? By swimming only. Willie was in a mood for risks. He pulled round the old mare short and set her at the hedge. She took it like a bird. Two fields off the river gleamed cold in moonlight. Seeing it the old mare cocked her ears thoughtfully, and glanced warningly back at her rider out of the corner of an eye. But he held her straight.

'That's all right old lady!' he cried, tightening his knees, and sitting well back. 'Do it your own way if you like: but we are going across!' And, 'I'm sorry I hit you' – he added.

Arrived at the bank there was a slight hesitation but no hint of refusal. Marigold wanted a good take off. That's all: but there wasn't one, so after scrambling down a little way, splash they went, falling almost headlong. Willie slipping off her back swam accom-panying his mount, and after being carried a little up stream (for the flow was tidal) they reached the bank together. It was he who first accomplished the landing by means of an overhanging willow. Then he helped the mare out. She was – poor thing – nearly spent. But a dripping messenger arrived quarter of an hour before a dry one could possibly have, and though it was all in vain Willie felt satisfied that he had done his best. Besides that the physical effort calmed the horror in his brain, and he jogged slowly home, after swallowing some brandy at the doctor's, with a mind that was once more normal.

His wild mood faded in the days that followed, but never entirely evaporated out of memory. Time, and especially the need to help others, heals all sorrows, though the scars remain.

But Time and the love of kind – these things also are of God's creation, and if the first impression never left him, it certainly mellowed, and obtained a fresh significance in his mind. Nor in the fullness of time did it lack that atmosphere of beauty which pity and thought bestow upon all human destiny.

In that new mood Willie, when the funeral flowers had withered, and the horses which his father had loved so well were taken away; with everything save the home, reserved for his mother, gone: wrote those lines which stand at the commencement of the previous chapter.

CHAPTER III

Soon after this, it was decreed by a doctor that a holiday should be taken by the two boys. Their father's death, and other things, had brought each within appreciable distance of a breakdown. Mrs. Harvey in her wonderful strength remained at home. She had doubtless felt the parting more keenly than either, but there are natures whose reserve of power seems never exhausted, and her's was one. People marvelled at her equanimity. She was apparently unchanged in body or soul by this new sorrow. She was not a stoic, and had never heard of Marcus Aurelius, but he would have loved her.

So in October the boys set off. They might have gone to France or Italy which was what the doctor advised, but he agreed that the best place for them to go was where they wanted.

'I would feel well on top of those hills', said Willie, pointing to the high smoky line of the Dean Forest. Eric didn't care where he went. So it was decided that for a fortnight, or longer if they wished, the brothers should walk over Gloucestershire hills amid the falling leaves.

The mind, which wounds the body, may heal it. The body which houses and feeds the mind may change it for better or worse. At the end of a fortnight they returned cured.

Whether it was the new air which entered their lungs, or whether it was the new decisions they took into their souls, which worked the magic, who can say? But as students of the latter rather than the former, it is with their talks rather than their travels that we are concerned though it must be admitted that the former as often as not arose out of the latter.

It is not necessary to make a guide-book itinerary of their walk but rather a hotch-pot of such memories as resulted. Nor was it always the same things which impressed them.

To Willie, a great event was their meeting with the garrulous Rabelaisian old shepherd at Newnham-on-Severn. Shepherd he called himself, and undoubtedly a number of his eighty-odd years had been spent tending sheep on the Cotswold hills where he was born, – 'nigh Ciciter'. But save a mere knowledge of flocks and their ailments makes the profession (as laymen might argue) and not rather an almost superstitious devotion to them (as experts maintain) the man was no shepherd. He was no man of the hills. He was a man of the world – spiritually, belike, a lesser thing; yet a much more entertaining one. He could talk, could this old one-toothed mortal! But his talk like Peter's, bewrayed him. For it was not of sheep, but (with a wicked twinkling) of woman shepherdesses 'under a barrow with the sun agin 'im'; of pheasants poached with sulphur burned under a roosting tree, or taken with raisins saturated in brandy: and the brandy ('come to that') was smuggled off boats at Newnham.

They sat all three in a barn. It was raining.

'There is no more pleasant sound in the world than rain drumming on thatch; – with you under it,' said Willie, as they watched grey sheets of water trailed shaking in the wind across the doorway. 'And no snugger spot nor a barn, whether fer sleepin' in or courtin' in' replied the ancient man. He looked like some disreputable old monk suddenly resurrected, where he sat cowled with a sack, in the semi-darkness.

'Ah, and you've tried both, I warrant.' said Willie.

Darkness chuckled. 'Seventy or sixty year ago', when labourers worked for 9d. a day, there'd be no lodging but barns for the extra haymakers and harvesters. Men and women, they all turned in together, making their beds in the straw 'snug enough'. But 'nowdays a chap ud be ashamed to say as a wer begot under barn-thatch, let alone borned there, as I've knowed 'em'…

'Those were bad old times' said Eric.

'Bad an' good as you mid zay. Zo all times be.'

Willie laughed.

'But surely', argued his brother, 'surely people are happier now, in better conditions, than they were then, living like beasts of the field.'

'They be aal on 'em flocking away into gurt black smokey towns nowdays.'

'But even so', interjected Eric, 'the conditions –'

'Beaasts in a pen', concluded the old countryman.

'And beaasts in a field be better off than beaasts in a pen', put in Willie. 'I agree. But did you ever work in the towns?' he asked.

'Did 'ee ever walk along the Thames embankment in Lonnon?' rejoined the ancient.

Wondering what was coming, the boys answered that on one occasion they had.

'Well, I helped put un wer a be, then', asserted this astonishing old fellow, and paused for the words to sink in.

'You helped build the embankment!' exclaimed the brothers, in voices which showed that they were sufficiently impressed.

'I helped put un wer a be'.

'And you didn't like the work?' enquired Eric.

The old man gave a chuckle. 'The work, ess I wer lucky in that. Ater dree days I dug up a gold piece. Tur's like a suverin only thinner; and twern't English. I took un to a shop, and a jew paid me dirty shillings down for't. Then me and my two mates got drunk wi the dirty shilling, and we was turned off.'

'So you were lucky' commented Willie smiling.

'Yes, I wer lucky. I come away from Lonnon, and I stayed away.' The old man deftly speared an onion with his single shaky tooth, and offered one onion each to the boys. Fumbling in his pockets for the bread and cheese he disclosed a dead rabbit which they affected not to see. 'Not many o' they in Lonnon', observed this merry old poacher.

The boys then asked him if he would walk as far as the village inn where they intended to get a meal, but the old man having both food and drink with him preferred to remain where he sat. He would see them there in the evening, and take a pint.

The boys looked at one another. They were not staying the night at Newnham. The rain had ceased. By evening they should be at least ten miles off. But this man (thought Willie) was a character – too good to lose. And here (thought Eric) was a man who had lived 80 years and was soon to go before his Maker. They exchanged glances, and each knew that the other was ready to sacrifice a meal.

Willie bit his onion. 'Then', said he, 'we'll bide here a bit if you will talk to us, for we're not staying out the evening.' The ancient nodded. 'I've a wonderful remembery', he said, 'and youngsters be glad to hear the things as did come about afore they was born; – not as yow be special young', he added courteously, as though youth were a sin to be ashamed of.

'You are an old man now', said Eric, 'what do you think of death?'

"Tis in the natur o' things' answered the poacher.

'How do you bite your food, now all your teeth but one are gone?' asked Willie.

'My gums be as rocky as tith, and I can chew with 'em as well as when tith was there, a'most. This un be a hindrance more nor a help', he added.

His wives were dead – 'two on 'em', and all his old friends; but he spoke as a man who had enjoyed living, and who still enjoyed it. there was no bitterness in his talk. His present master was a good 'un, but inclined to hurry. He never hurried, and no good varmer didn't. There was a time for everything, and then one should do it. He liked work and he liked sport – not football and such like games. They wasted a man's time, and didn't bring them in nothing either.

He talked of his ferrets which were in great demand during 'rab-butting time'. Conventional honesty was hardly a strong point with him, for he related with an infinite relish of the jest (even when it turned against himself) how when one of his 'verruts' had died, he having provided the ferret's body with shot marks, took it out on three successive 'shoots', and was paid its value twice over by sports-men who believed that they had killed it in firing at a rabbit. He might, he added, have been paid on a third occasion but that 'the verrut had begun to stink, and maaster smelt un.'

Eric's laugh equalled his brother's in loud enjoyment, and the old man's topped both ...

This was at Newnham-on-Severn. Some days after, Eric talking to gypsies on Wigpool common, learnt of the existence and where-abouts of that cave called 'Christ a-weeping'.

They were now on almost the highest ridge of those forested hills:– 'ringed with the azure world.' Tall Cotswolds lay like a faint blue trail of smoke along the sky twenty or thirty miles to east. Westward there towered irregularly and yet more phantom-like the mountains of Wales. May Hill, covered with bracken, rose suddenly like a rusty gigantic bubble of earth less than a league away; and closer still, the pasture and plough of Herefordshire spread a little patchwork quilt of fertile country over the near landscape. The fire-made rocks of Malvern shaped themselves unmistakably, zigzagged upon the middle distance.

The forest itself frittered away into bushes on the summit called Wigpool Common, and here alone among the holies and the yews camped gypsies in a spot dangerously pitted with ancient iron-work-ings partially overgrown.

An unusual intimacy was permitted the boys by these pictur-esque and suspicious people when they discovered that they and swarthy friends to wit:– Bartholomew Fury and Elijah Dark – had on occasions bought and sold horses from and to their father and grandfather at Barton Fair. A girl whose dark remarkable beauty haunted him for weeks after, told Willie his fortune which was, upon her showing, to remain for ever a stranger to riches, and to marry a foreigner. Eric's fortune she gravely professed herself unable to predict. She took no part in the brothers' chaff of one another, but later initiated them into the art of basket making, and showed them how to cook a hedgehog by rolling it into a dumpling of clay which was then deposited amongst embers of glowing fire-wood. The baked clay being removed carried away the creature's inedible spikes, and revealed a hot and savoury dinner, which the boys tasted, and to their surprise liked.

It was at her suggestion that they visited Christ a-weeping, and her father showed them the way. Otherwise they would hardly, even by the most explicit directions, have found it.

In one of the many holes roofed with red-berried yew, there bubbled from tall rock a tiny spring of water spilling over in the life-sized shape of a man from whose face and robes tears dropped eternally down into the basin grooved by their ceaseless falling upon an iron surface.

"Tis Christ a-weeping' said the gypsy.

In the gloom of the cavern the boys stood and regarded that strange and impressive symbol of God mourning – lonely in the world He would save. Outside fell the sunshine lighting the berries of scarlet and splintering upon the branches. Hawks hovered. Wood pigeons cooed. A bell tinkled on the neck of a forest sheep dangerously straying. A faint continuous hum of insect life entered fitfully upon the breeze …

The best talk is at the end of a day's tramp. The body's juices are settled: the mind clear – full like a pool of clear water with the reflections of light and sun. Even in dull country, by virtue of mere physical exercise, does this miracle occur; and when the walk has been lovely as well as strenuous the beauty of the way is absorbed unconsciously by the mind leaving it clean of every-day humours and poisons.

Peace of the forest had for eight hard days deeply penetrated the souls of these brothers. There is nothing more restful than windy trees. In restfulness that sound surpasses the lap of the sea; the flicker of firelight; the muffled drumming of rain on thatch: the little delicious soft cough of it into the eave-butt. 'Peace! Peace! – the whole forest seems to sigh it' said Willie, listening to the voices of the trees which almost brushed the panes of their window at a small Inn – about the centre of ten square miles of whispering leafage.

'But who harbours it?' asked Eric. 'Which of the men in my bank, in your office, in the cities around, or in the forest itself, keeps it in his heart? Who harbours it?'

'Who? – None!' was the reply. 'I know them, When they are not feverishly employed in making money, they are feverishly engaged in spending it.'

'And that', said Eric, 'is what we shall do in time. That is what we must do unless we change our ways: unless we are daring ... soon' he added.

So the cat was out. Often in their talks during this walking her leaf-green eyes had peered at them from the bag. Often her scratching had been audible in forest glades. She was out.

'There are two ways of living', went on Eric, 'one (and I believe not the best) possible only to a few daring spirits who will pay the price – the honest pagan life of men like your beloved shepherd of Newnham-on-Severn; accepting experience rough and smooth joyously or at least without regret and faced at last as by a blank wall with death: the other (better, and though hard, possible I believe to all) – the honest Christian; transmuting experience by belief, and looking beyond the wall at the end. You and I in the life we lead are neither. The whole present age is neither. The people you and I live with since we left childhood, and the farm, cannot live. They cannot be happy. They cannot know peace. And we shall get like them. Don't think I am superior in talking like this, It is God who gives truth, and He alone gives faith, and the peace that comes from it. But the truth is that not one of us dares grasp happiness: dares grasp peace, by reason of a cowardly allegiance to the world as he finds it – a world which dare neither accept life in the pagan way nor live it in the Christian.'

'It is true' said Willie.

'Peace', went on his brother, 'comes in the acceptance of life as it is without explanations: with no reasons, if with occasional rhymes – a hard creed, a dispiriting and debasing one: or peace comes gloriously in zest of service which enables one to disregard present hardships because the end is noble. To live nobly is to do the work (whatever it be) that God meant us to do.'

'It is hard to be sure what that is' said Willie.

'Yes, old man, it takes a long fight to find that out; and, as I admitted, it takes daring in the fight. But a time comes when to our own human gnawing hunger for something (a hunger which may deceive us) there comes, as there has come in these last few days of walking in the forest, a conviction imposed.'

'As though the trees had voices, and talked of God – openly', said Willie.

'Ah, you have heard that too!'

'I have; and I am glad you have spoken now. I was frightened somehow at what they said. I, whose passion it is to make poems – I did not know how to begin to speak of it. And now', concluded Willie, 'and now, it has come, and what (think of everything) are we to do?'

Eric wrinkled his brows. 'It is difficult I know', he said, 'difficult: but once we have glimpsed light and freely given ourselves to follow, God will provide a path. Yes, I am sure of that', he added.

So, the boys grasped hands and turned to sleep …

'Why do you want to write poetry?' asked Eric an evening later. (Now that is a hard question if you like!) Willie thought.

'I have tried prose', he answered, 'but my best thoughts always run into verse:– not that I mean it to', he reflected. (A good reply!) 'For somehow', he went on, 'the building up of a poem (and every poem is built:– constructed upon the original bit of inspiration supplied free, somehow this building takes the original meaning which is our (quickly forgotten) sight of God's gift, and makes it better than it was.'

(Full marks for Willie, who has perceived that miracle which form alone imposes!)

'I don't understand how', he admitted. (Who does?)

'God is a capitalist who supplies the materials, but poets must always be labourers', he explained. Eric nodded assent.

'This I do know, however; and understand', he continued, 'poetry is not the finnicking pastime of rich people (which the world supposes) but something common to all men:– as feeding as bread and cheese. Bread nourishes the body. Song satisfies a common hunger of the soul.'

'Then it is like religion', said Eric.

'It is. It is religion.'

They had crossed the Severn at Arlingham and were following the shining horse-shoe bend of it to Framilode where they meant to sleep. Another day's walk would see them home.

'The ideal poem' continued Willie, 'is magical as Coleridge and Keats; as accessible as Wordsworth and Whiteman.'

'That', thought Eric, 'was what Christianity should be.' 'So now', he added, 'we are both enlisted under the banner of the Holy Ghost. May Christ help us!'

'God's world, for me!' cried Willie. He was watching the fishermen mending nets beside water rose and gold with sunset – 'Christ's empire for you!'

'Amen!'

'Burns was not a very great writer', mused Willie, later, 'but he was one of the very happiest (or should be if he can see the world), for his songs are read and sung by common people. I want Gloucestershire people – fishermen and shepherds – to sing my songs. I want them to shake the beams of Inns. I want ploughmen to shout them. Then I would be happy' ...

A half-timbered Inn with red blinds sheltered them at Framilode. Shelter – what shelter does man need from light of stars shaping themselves to immemorial patterns in immemorial skies: from rainy sounding trees and yellow windows peering through with so friendly a human look! What shelter should be craved from sea winds scented with country travel: from an echo across water which thrice-speaks music of singing men: a tearing sound of tide rushing past for a full hour and gradually diminishing, till after a time of silence in which you may hear your watch ticking the delicious moments, it turns again to the sea! What shelter from a curve of moonlit river: shadowy hills from whence it flows: a belated bird singing on Barrow Hill; and moon bright piratical spits of sand – the prey of tides! It was there they slept.

At dawn they rose. Fog had not then lifted its white curtain upon the drama of human life. Yellow elm tops made islands in a moving ocean of mist, milk white. Timid animals were creeping to their dens and holes. The sun arose. Dew glinted in bare hedges and hung upon pointed thorn. A horse, shod golden in sunrise, rolled in grey meadows, waving his legs. Then Man went 'forth to his work and labour until the evening.'

One offered the boys a place in his boat. It was only occasionally that one could journey from Framilode to Minsterworth by water. He was going to do it on 'three quarter tide':– grasping as it were the mane of the great wave which would take them safely over the wide and shallow stretch of Bollo against the flow of Severn.

They jumped at the opportunity. The bore foamed past. They gave it a good start. Then the trouble of water following, the boat was boarded and put adrift. 'Steady – sit quiet!' She is heading for Minsterworth, and (what fun!) away they go on a body of roving sea water journeying home – home again! ...

> 'Prince, you have horses: motors, I suppose
> As well! At finding pleasure you're no fool.
> But have you got a little boats that blows
> Up-stream from Framilode to Bollopool?'

Cotswold towered before them her quarries white in the morning. Behind were the Forest hills from which they had travelled. They are riding the tide like a grey horse cantering easily:

> 'And round the boat the broken water crows
> With laughter casting pretty ridicule
> On human life and all its little woes
> Up-stream from Framilode to Bollopool.'

It was in trenches that Willie wrote his 'Ballade of River Sailing' and with later memories of Severn in mind, but the germ of that poem took life surely in these swift moments, with Eric sitting silent and thrilled in the boat beside him, as they danced upon the water.

At home that night they lay long awake talking of all that had happened to them on the holiday which was now over: discussing from all standpoints the decisions they had made in that old Forest of Dene, and which must now be carried into effect.

Willie broached the matter in characteristic fashion by handing his brother a slip of dirty paper scrawled over with verses. Eric looked at it, and smiled 'You must decipher it for me, old man!'

'It is the poem', said Willie, 'that I have been hammering out during our tramp home. It's about the forest: what it seemed to say to both of us – "Peace!" So "In the Forest" is the title of it. It came to me so poignantly that the trees or rather their far ancestors had uttered that word ages and ages ago before any man was there to listen. They have never ceased to say it over. And now man is here:– man for whose sake they were taught to speak it. But he won't listen! It is as if the whole world were dead!'

'Read the poem', said Eric in reply, and his brother did so.

We have come out of the world
Under the green banners of peace
Unfurled:
For the world is dead.
Peace! peace! peace!
Over and over let the sweet word be said.
Long long before tongue spoke
This rustling soft word of the trees
Awoke!
No one was there to listen and understand
What the trees said, the trees
Of that weird lonely land.
And 'peace' – that tragic-sweet word
Yet in a dead world's ear
Is whispered.
Aye, though green flags of peace
Are flying in victory near
Man lies defeated: and trees
Ever – ever unheard
Over the world do sigh
The word:
And wave tempestuous sunny banners of Peace
In triumph high
Unseen – save of living trees!

'It is an experiment technically' he went on. 'I have tried by repetition of sybilant rhymes, half-rhymes, and use of suspended rhythms to reproduce the whispering of a forest. Of course it has not "come off" all through. It is skating on thin ice. But I don't see how else it is to be done', he concluded.

'It is a good poem', said Eric, – and believed it. 'I cannot give you one in return. But I will try and live mine.'

'And now, old pal', said his brother, some moments later, 'we've got to tell mother' ...

The next evening they did it – and she (the wise sweet woman) understood.

First let Willie pass his final examination was her counsel. He would so at least have a sound profession to fall back on if the world – as was its fashion – should batter the artist. Poverty's loaded dice would not so easily triumph. That was true, and both boys agreed.

Eric, she said, would be as well (or badly) off in a rectory as in a bank. So there was no need for him to delay. A mortgage should provide the necessary training as soon as that could be arranged. Then they must fight their ways ('and God be with you my dears!') in the battle they had chosen.

'You only can know whether it is the service God meant you to do', she concluded. 'We must all serve, and fight hard to be happy.'

Now that was a queer and illuminating saying from one whose goodness seemed to be so absolutely effortless. But that also was true.

PART IV

TEMPTATION

CHAPTER I

So now after twelve chapters we have arrived at that point where most novels begin. So far as have merely seen what made the boys. We now turn to observe what the world, and the war did to them. So far the influences have necessarily been particular in character since they went to form two particular personalities. What in essence happened to them may have happened to no others. But now the influences will be general. What now comes happens to millions of others besides our two boys:– happens to all. The effects may be different (indeed if they were not there would be no need to write novels) but the things are always the same. The material of life shapes ever to the old patterns. Men dream dreams and are disillusioned finding or failing to find at last the dream which awaits no disillusion. A man strives and fails and rises again embittered or sweetened by his fall. He knows curiosity. He knows adventure. He know fear. He meets friends only to part with them. He learns the magic and value of memory which so encircles and tortures a man. He falls into love and risks many things driven by it. He falls into folly and into sin and learns their natures. He is made homesick at a word: at another he flames into murder. He cries in agony to God and to his fellows and they seem deaf. Pride and humility – those best and the worst of human emotions play upon him with discord or harmony. Gratitude, the twin sister of Humility, sweetens his bread. Common life seems at times most wonderful, and at times intolerable. This it is to have been born a man. The world brings such to all – take them or leave them. It is life.

But it is the meeting of man with life (in a clash of steel and flint) which lights the spark of romance. There is no romance without man to make it. This has been romance in all times – man fighting. The old romance concerned itself with men dead or living (but defiant) confronting the forces of nature. Against odds tremendous he died gallant or merely pathetic. The outer world, Nature, grim Death, gaunt Hunger, all aching impossible things he faced and dying handed on the torch of defiance. His victories increased. The tide of battle turned against the blind giants. Nature, that terrible foe, became tame: cringed dog-like before him. In the last century both steam and electricity turned to lashes in his hand:–

'Glory to man in the highest
For Man is the master of things!'

Sang the poet of that age. It seemed that the battle was done.

Then Romance became a butt of the intellectuals, who thought it dead. They thought narrowly. Man had more enemies than he knew:– more than were visible. His old eternal enemy lives. That which laughed at his vain assault upon the mastodon: which gloated when the careless teeth of Frost gnawed the thin thread of life to which he held: which clapped hands above the grave of its puny yet unconquerable foe: That dies not! When that dies, it will be the end of the world, and not until that dies will Romance be dead.

For Romance is wherever men fight the immemorial battle of their fathers and of their sons. It is there whatever be the result of the battle. It feeds not on achievement, but on hope.

The new Romance (if you will have it so) does not war against flesh and blood, 'but against principalities and powers, and against spiritual wickedness in high' (and low) 'places'. Subdue earth and the stars; that battle will still rage on! It is the old war, though the Accuser has called new battalions into action. It is the old war. When it will end, God alone knows. How, we doubt not, and must not doubt, if we are men. That faith only is our birthright ...

In the early part of the year 1913, between Christmas and twelfth night, ere holly and the milky-berried mistletoe had ceased to reign over firelight and good cheer, in any old-fashioned house, there sat one evening in a small ring around the fire, Mrs. Harvey and her two sons talking and munching apples in candle-light.

Something more than twelve moths have passed since the events and decisions related in the previous chapter. Eric is now an undergraduate, and 'down' on his first vacation. His brother has with some pains qualified as a solicitor of the Supreme Court of Judicature – a sounding title! It amuses him.

'Tomorrow,' says he, turning over the orange envelope of a telegram, 'as a solicitor of the Supreme Court of Judicature, I shall travel in a panting train to an ugly manufacturing town in the Midlands: because like Caliban, "I must eat my dinner"'.

'Dinner is always here, for you, dear,' put in his mother gently.

'It poisons me since I have not paid for it.'

'Dearest!'

'Darling, I don't mean to be unkind, but it is true. It was true even of the poor old cock we had for supper tonight. (Alas poor Yorick. I knew him well. A fellow of infinite jest!) He was so tall and bright with his red comb and his coloured tail. He was lovely and pleasant in his life, but in his death he was divided. And he dug his spurs into Dolly when she caught him:–

(Singing) 'And red blood flowed all round all round
O the red blood flowed all round.'

But I digress. Man cannot pick up corn like cocks do. He cannot eat grass like red and white cows ...

My heart is with those shaggy colts

Who lounge in meadows gold and green:– How's that for the beginning of a lyric? Shell I continue? – No, poetry is now a subject taboo!'

'Why? You are in such good form to-night,' said Eric falsely, out of fellowship.

'Good form? Tomorrow, as I said before, I shall be a Solicitor of the Supreme Court of Judicature; and I shall go by train for the purpose of examining deeds relating to land which I shall never see:– pearled with dew and daisies, and gleaming here and there with such pools as flash past that railway carriage. I shall hear with interest at Assizes how that Titania Lewin Bottom did after attempting to drown one William Lewin Bottom with intent in so doing feloniously wilfully and of malice aforethought him to kill and murder, herself on the blank day of blank unlawfully throw and cast into certain water within the borough, called the canal with intent thereby feloniously wilfully and of her malice aforethought to kill and murder whom? Why, herself again! And she all skin and grief as Trigg hath it.'

'The poor creatures!' cried Mrs. Harvey laughing and at the same time looking within a measurable distance of tears.

'Perhaps you will go there to defend the said Who-was-it Bottom – poor woman,' suggested Eric.

'It is in my bones that I shall prosecute,' replied his brother, 'but we will hope for the best:– and coming to think of it,' he added, 'the latter would perhaps be her best chance of escape. I am sorry (in a different tone) to have to entertain my two best friends with humour of this forced trivial kind, but what will you, dears? It is better to jest (however poorly) than to weep, which is what I feel like doing whenever I remember the last six months.'

'Poor darling – you'll succeed yet!' cried his mother.

'Everyone has had to go through this at their beginnings,' comforted Eric. 'Courage old man! You can't expect to make a living by writing straight off.'

'I was a fool to try, no doubt,' began Willie.

'Not to try, but certainly to despair,' was the answer.

'It's all right for you to preach –'

'I'm not. I didn't mean that.'

'I'm sorry, old man. I know you didn't. Only listen – You can't understand. However hard your grind and your doubts, you are on your way. Every step takes you nearer the goal. But I – Fate or Nature or something has scratched me for the event.'

'Don't talk in that way, my dear. It is –'

'Mate, I suppose. Well, let it be mate,' he answered his mother. 'Anyway what the devil is Nature playing at? If I can't write, why must I keep on? For six months I have been sending things to papers –'

'Six months,' broke in Eric, 'but what is six months?'

'It was the work of five years, filed and revised, tested in sunlight and moonlight. What is it Whitman says? Anyway it was work, real work, such as any sweating navvy knows, any lumberman. The editors regretted it, etcetera. Then, thought I, still believing in myself – as (against evidence) I still do (he added defiantly); then I thought "perhaps it is because I do not know London, and how to "do it." – I will get an agent. So I sent my stuff to "the Camford Literary Agency," who took the money, and later replied, "We herewith return your MSS. which we regret, etc. etc." The list of typed refusals took up about two pages. Then what the devil, I repeat, is Nature playing at? I gave up. At times I ceased to believe in myself. And if I, then who?'

'But we have not,' said his mother in a challenging tone.

'I decided that I would at least live honestly. I would pay my way. I would be a Solicitor of the Supreme Court of Judicature. And, behold, thanks to my good parents I was that already! So I am.'

'But –'

'But it is time to go to bed. I must catch that train tomorrow,' he ended, – and arose.

'Goodnight, dearest,' said his mother, as he kissed her. 'There is another poet – a king and a sinner as are we all – whose words are in my heart tonight.' He paused on his way out. 'It is only a bit of the poem that I remember, but all that he wished his friend, I wish to my dear son – that God will (these are the words) 'grant thee thy heart's desire" (thy heart's desire, my son) "and fulfill all thy mind" ...

'It is a good wish, and a kind wish, dear,' said he. 'Good-night, mother!'

'Good-night, old man!'

After he had gone, Mrs. Harvey said, 'I'm anxious about Willie, dear.'

'Why, Mother?'

'He is not like you,' began his mother.

'He has a lot more brains, and a lot more pluck, in some ways.'

'In some ways, true; but they are not the right ways; not the happy ways. I know him. I bred him. I am his mother. As a little boy it was the same, and it always will be. He could never wait' ... The light of candles flickering, and firelight painted their grave faces.

'He has got courage, Mother.'

'Yes, but there are two kinds of courage. There is the courage of daring – a gay, valiant thing, and lovely to look at. He has got that. He had it as a baby when he would gulp the nastiest medicine with a smile. But there is courage of another kind – a grimmer, less dramatic sort that lies in endurance. Willie can't endure.' A log spurted purple flame and died black.

'If you could see him go through a ninety minute football match,' began Eric.

'That is physical. It is the strong body he inherits. What I mean is that the soul, which is his own, has no – what shall I say? – Hope. I can't explain. But I know. His daring and his gaiety is a sort of brave glitter on despair.

'Poor boy! I believe you are right. Willie is pagan at bottom. He does not feed on God as we all must, but on dreams that give no suck. He talks about God's world, but it is hard to know what he means by it, for he seldom speaks of God Himself, and still seldomer of Christ – our only Comforter.'

'God knows many men who do not know Him,' replied the mother.

'Yes, dear, and He will tend him and lead him to Himself, for He loves every one of His children.'

'I know that, dear. I am only anxious for Willie because he is my little son, too. And he is going to be very unhappy while he is finding out.'

'He is so seldom unhappy. I never had better company than his.'

'And that is not a good thing,' said this wise woman. 'It is better sometimes to be unhappy,' she added.

'How?'

'It is the only natural road to joy. There is a pride in being persistently gay. It is as though a man said he could make life better than God – but no one can. And the thing we call unhappiness is part of life. I mean that it is to be endured, not ignored.'

'You are a wise old woman, dearest.'

'And now,' (smiling) said Mrs. Harvey, 'I remember a very quaint little trick of Willie's when he was a baby – before you were born. That too was characteristic. He had a habit of shutting his eyes, and simply blotting out the world when he did not like it. It was very funny. "The poor mite is tired," people said, when he did it in the middle of their attentions to him. And, "I think he is," I used to answer – but that was not what they meant. I knew that he had no desire to go to sleep. I knew he was just bored.'

Eric laughed.

'And so he shut his eyes. And he is the same now. He can't endure, I mean. He just refuses to be bored' …

'Surely that is a virtue – isn't it?'

'Only (gravely) if you are strong enough to accept – all. How few there are who can do that!'

'It is hard, indeed,' said Eric.

CHAPTER II

'When I am living in the Midlands
That are sodden and unkind –'

The letters which Willie wrote from his new abode offered little contradiction to those anticipated judgments. They showed no trace of boredom, but a good many of central unhappiness.

Eccleton was (he wrote) just another of those black and accursed towns glorified by Arnold Bennet. Its extreme ugliness was excelled only by its absurd sense of civic importance. It was (like his employer) self made, and vain of the fact, though the work in neither case seemed worth doing. The occupation of his first landlady was apparently that of a married woman living apart from her husband. His second landlady was a kindly soul aged fifty whose passion was for cats and hot whiskey.

Coal was cheap owing to the proximity of mines, and was very necessary in that atmosphere of dampness and gloom – 'not more' (said he) 'for the dispelling of the first than the cheerful painting of the second. What a joy is fire! I am tempted to write an essay upon it. Or a poem. Or both. Nobody would ever read them, but I should have paid my debt to the fierce and friendly thing when I had cast the manuscripts into its golden devouring mouth.

It is (he writes) more often wet than not wet here, but one never hears the music of rain. Where is that sweet lisp in grass and garden; where the hoofs of those faery horses that gallop on thatch; and splendid and gusty drumming upon windows facing wide windy spaces; the little giggle and cough of water falling into eave-butts? What passes here for rain is no more than fog and smuts dissolved in filthy dew.'

To live here after Minsterworth, he wrote, is like stepping out of a poem by Chaucer into a novel by Zola.

'As to the people all Eccleton is divided into three parties (vide Caesar's Commentaries) who are now in the throes of an election petition. The parties are termed Conservatives, Radicals, and Socialists.

The first is, as Mr. Mantelini would say, "a demmed moist unpleasant body," the second equally unpleasant but less moist; the third no more pleasant or less demmed, but noisier than the other two put together.

The petition is by the Radicals, but the Conservatives make counter charges of bribery. (It is as though one five year old corpse should charge another with corruption!) I am collecting evidence for the Conservative party. We are, it seems, guilty of slipping sovereigns into whiskey till it is "strong enough." They prefer to insert notes into bibles. It is all a matter of principle and belief. the third party, having no money, for the most part contents itself with taking what the others have to give, and then voting the opposite way. Observe that all this arises out of an annual squabble called the municipal elections, and is nothing to do with parliament! The work is rather fun', he concludes. What he finds nauseous is having to prosecute poor men for money-lenders.

He tells how on one occasion having gone into a mean street with a County Court summons for money due to such an one of his principal's clients, he came upon a dazed anaemic-looking woman in the midst of five small filthily dirty children, and tried to explain that her husband must pay 'by Saturday' a certain sum of money or else have judgment given against him; and that this would be followed by the selling up of their dirty home – execution seemed too fine a word. Now this case could hardly have been twisted even by a Communist to serve as an example of social injustice. The by no means admirable usurer was by every convenient or unconventional meaning of the word a better man than the weak and dishonest sot who had come willingly (with his family) into the web. But the squalor of the place; the dazed and dumb stupidity of the woman surrounded with her crying filthy children, filled him suddenly with rage against the universe. 'Oh, hell! never mind all that now,' he shouted. 'Tell your husband, when he comes home, that I have paid the nine pounds for him. You understand –' The woman certainly did not. She looked at him in the same dumb, bestial silence. 'You understand!' he shouted, 'you arn't to worry any more! You'll hear no more about it.'

There was no charity in the act, as he himself admitted, (though in the state of his pocket there was certainly sacrifices; for nine pounds was a lot to pay) but anything to get out of this atmosphere, away from people like this! That was the thought in his mind, – sheer disgust at the root of it.

He was murderously angry (and so was his employer) when their client, the money lender, got to hear of the affair because the dolt who had benefited went boasting his fortune and flinging it in the face of his late creditor, though never a word of thanks had marked his acceptance of the gift.

What (asks Willie) can you do with people like this? They have no breeding in them; no courtesy, no manners. Compared to that old shepherd at Newnham, to Bill Trigg, to Tater Baggit even, they are just mongrel curs. Oh, God, I wish – I wish I were dead, or back in Gloucestershire.

Shortly after this outburst Willie's letters became more cheerful – but told a good deal less. Why?

It is the privilege of the novelist (as of the modern biographer) to know the thoughts of his characters, and to reveal, if he chose, what they themselves think too hateful to tell to the world. But for the present we need range no further than over that little pile of private reflections written down in the diary he revived during this unhappy period, for no other reason, we suppose, than that which causes any diary of reflections to be kept by lonely people throughout the world.

There is a certain strain of morbidity in these writings which suggests that he was not only spiritually but physically ill. Suicide is a recurring motif in a theme of seldom-silenced despair.

In reading we must remember that he was young. That the world was not built a play-ground, and has been turned by man into something far different, is in youth a fact somehow incomprehensible. Elders are very hard on young people. The young man does not know even – himself. The old man knows no one else. It is a miserable thing to be out of heaven, with all the earth against one.

Remember also that he had wiser man than he (or you gentle reader) before him in this immortal debate of 'To be or not to be'. That greatest Dean of St. Paul's, John Donne, and long before him Epectitus had cast their votes upon the unorthodox – they who knew life well, the great Christian and the great pagan.

The subject is introduced by jotting from the latter. 'If things begin to pall on you, retire; but if you stay do not complain.' It was a precept Willie had always obeyed by instinct. He had never complained. He never would. But that he felt very much like retiring the next entry shows:– 'Must I forfeit the right to address a C of E parson in heaven (or wherever they go)? Certainly they will deny me a place in holy ground for burial. Holy ground! (Dear, dear mother Earth!) They will call me a coward – they who never risked life for anything in heaven or earth! A fool perhaps ... We try in vain to unravel the threads of life. But they are greater fools to whom life has no tangled threads. Is a man a coward because he refuses to fondle a toad? What else is life such as this? Is it not braver to face the lion? The suicide is not frightened. He is disgusted. Death he dares. Only life he will not tolerate.'

Then a reflection – 'I would have spared Mother this. Well, perhaps we shall meet again somewhere – and she will understand.'

then a memory – 'How lovely are birds – that little mouse-like thing that runs along branches for insects, how often I have watched him upon the oak at home. Robin like an old English squire: that speckled singer, the thrush. Sparrows the most impudent of all. And those black pirates the crows. This morning (in town!) a bird whistled so queerly, and then he called out some droll suggestion and laughed What! What! and fled away to the woods. The robin takes himself more seriously. His little tender message of beauty is given again and again in careful crystalline phrase. As the tiny mumruffin – Ah, dear memory – (the paragraph here breaks off).

And now perhaps the time has come to avail ourselves of our novelist's prerogative, revealing what actually and in secret happened of all this.

Dwelling in Eccleton – a queerly coloured orchid amidst thistles and lesser things – was a lady by name of Mrs. Violet Bransbury-Stuart, inhabiting a large and luxurious house with a bald-headed bullying J.P. called Bransbury-Stuart who owned coal mines. She was young – thirty to be exact – and wanton; yet more human than most of those who held her anathema.

The Eccleton canal winds – a dirty thing – through slums, and past 'Highfield' the house inhabited by Mr. and Mrs. Violet Bransbury-Stuart on the outskirts of the town. There is a towpath skirting the canal. It was of use to Mrs. Bransbury-Stuart on occasions as a short and hidden way home, there being no lights upon it other than stars faintly reflected in the black water.

Passing hastily that way one night in the last summer which preceded the Great War, she was startled by a splash as of some heavy thing being thrown into the water a short distance off.

Pluck was not wanting to her equipment and she was on the spot in time to drag from the water and revive a dripping man whose hands were bound tightly with cord.

It was but a few yards further to 'Highfield' and there she took him. The cords which had marked his wrists she threw away. And the gentleman who had accidentally fallen into the canal; and was then and there warmed with brandy, comforted with fire, and re-apparelled in dry though ill-fitting clothes belonging to her husband, was (so it turned out) a young solicitor of the town, by name of Harvey.

CHAPTER III

'No siren this – a woman
Whose way was ever gay,
Half honest, wholly human,
She goes her sunlit way
As in Boccacio's day.

In her all frailty
Doth seem a pretty folly,
Nor is she enemy
To aught save melancholy:
And to – mankind may-be.'

Dainty china tinkled. Silver gleamed. Steaming water bubbled above a little blue and yellow flame which flickered in a fantastic blossom beneath it. clear amber liquid became cloudy with cream. Mrs. Bransbury-Stuart – a queen in her small kingdom – poured out tea.

Six months had passed since that first unconventional meeting between herself and Willie – now the sole quest – and they had come to know one another 'rather well'.

Yet 'rather well' was not well enough to at least one of them; – possibly both. 'Rather anything' was a term unsuited to either temperament. They did not so constrain emotion. Life meant something more than 'rather' to each of them.

But life means different things to different people. And these were very different people. Life had not hitherto satisfied Mrs. Bransbury-Stuart in this small matter. A queer reticence on Willie's part had prevented it. It was a reticence which, though fascinating, she had determined to remove.

During tea the talk was a good deal less significant than their thoughts, being occupied and exclusively with 'commonplace,' and conventional topics. Their minds if accessible must have exhibited matter at once more interesting and less edifying. (Here, one is tempted to ask, 'What in the name of goodness would happen to society in general if everybody (being an author) could see clearly the thoughts of all around?' It would dissolve like moisture in sunlight! It would break like a politician's promise! It is fortunate that no such uncomfortable thing has happened, or is likely to happen – even to authors.)

'And will the merman take more tea?' This pet name always offended Willie, who did not like to be reminded of that evening. Violet was cruelly aware of the fact. Cruelty is one of the most effective of sexual traps, though it requires skilful setting. Hate is not only better to win than indifference, it is often as good as love. There is moreover great satisfaction in hurting the thing one desires.

'No, thanks.'

'But he shall! That fascinating little scowl which he puts on, makes him' (taking and filling his cup) 'more like a merman than ever – A queer ugly babyish inhuman "old thing," he is come up through his own dark wandering element to see the world. He blinks at is so funnily. He cannot understand it at all. Let me tell your fortune, merman!' She reached across the table (flashing, as she knew how, the emeralds on her pretty fingers) to take his hand.

'No, you must come closer. Move your chair up to me.'

Willie obeyed. 'But I've had my fortune told before. I am going to be poor always, and I am going to marry a foreigner.'

'Oh, it doesn't matter whom you marry!' she replied significantly, looking back at him out of those queer slanting eyes which reminded him somehow of Clemmy's. 'Though as a matter of fact you shouldn't marry,' she added.

'Why?'

'Because it isn't worth while – for a man.'

'It is for a woman?'

'It is a protection and a screen to her. He does not need these.'

'Screen against what?' he asked.

'The eyes of the world,' was the reply.

'But,' began he – (This sort of talk had continued for three months – and seemed to her likely to do so for three more).

'Oh, never mind – "but"! I'm waiting to tell your immediate fortune.' Her knee slid by accident against his. If it exerted a slight pressure, which provoked in Willie a small but imperceptible shiver it was clearly without the knowledge of its owner. There are women who possess an uncanny power of unconsciousness regarding the movement of their limbs.

But Willie had an appointment. He was sorry, but his time would not permit the telling of his fortune.

Mrs. Bransbury-Stuart bit her lip as he arose. 'Then perhaps you can hear it this evening. Come to dinner. My husband will, I fear, be away, but –'.

Willie promised that he would be back at seven o'clock. Why? He did not himself know. Perhaps he wanted to. Perhaps he was lonely. Perhaps – Anyway he consented. To play with fire is a very human pastime, and Willie was human in spite of the description given of him as a merman.

'She is very like Clemmy – in some ways,' he thought as he departed. It was true. Those eyes, that bobbed hair, and the atmosphere which surrounded her, all combined to make convincing the subtle resemblance between two women whose superficial differences were evident. For Clemmy was dark, and she gloriously golden. Clemmy's eyes were like sloes, but her's the shifting colour of sea-water. the little, shabbily dressed, nursemaid had only one leg, but Violet Bransbury-Stuart (as the cut of her fashionable skirt amply proved) suffered from no such physical defect. She had two legs. And yet –

'Tonight she'll expect me to kiss her,' he mused; 'anyway I shall –' (This anticipation was as it happened a modest estimate of reality).

That lady, as she watched him depart, reassured herself with the memory of a shiver. Sensuality – she could play airs and variations upon the single string as well as any! It was the strings of his mind that she could not touch. That was always preoccupied with – Something. (Yes, even now Something was there, and speaking louder than any voices of Despair and Loneliness and Lust). She could not, she found, appropriate that, but his body was, she felt, already hers. Only the indirect method must go. By that sign – the shiver – she knew that her appeal must be to the passions alone, and also that any plain frontal attack would now succeed. It was of course to be taken for granted that the first victory would pay for all. There would be no difficulty after. She smiled prettily to herself in a mirror.

Firelight made a halo of her golden curls as she sat that night at dinner with Willie opposite. Gold of a paler colour lay in the half emptied glass she fingered. Golden bubbles uprise in a tiny tree from the glass's stem and spread upon the wine's surface in foamy foliage of gold. But her white hands lay bare in the lamp light; fingers uncircleted by any gold. Even the third finger of her left hand was bare.

They chatted lightly of this and that over the dessert. Then, rising, 'I have a present to show you,' she said. 'It is from an old friend' ('lover' thought Willie) 'of mine. He went East last year,' she added. 'And he had sent this,' picking up a tiny packet from the Chesterfield. Ribbons were untied, and a gauzy web of something flung to float like sunny mist upon the air.

'By Jove! – but what in the world is this beautiful thing?' cried Willie.

'A kimona.'

The shining mist moved slowly down and hung suspended from her bare arm which gleamed through. It was as though some great artist had of merest air woven this magic veil overwrought with bright ghosts of all strange birds and flowers that in his imagination sang and blossomed.

'But is – is this woven air to be worn?' he stammered.

'You shall see,' she replied as with a joyous smile she disappeared.

Her reappearance after a few moments was a reminder to Willie of the famous 'Prima vere' of Botticelli. With a scent of flowers Spring incarnate, Spring whose white body fought through and conquered its floating veil of breeze and bird-song; danced in, and stood before him. He sprang forward, and as he did so she flashed round and was gone, leaving him in an empty room. For an instant he faced the slammed door, hesitating. Then leaping forward as from a trance he followed through the darkness of the hall and sound of those retreating footsteps. At the end of the passage before a room flickering with fantastic firelight he paused since all guiding sounds had ceased. He entered the room. It was furnished cosily and luxuriously. A Bechstein piano reflected in its polished wood and face of fire whose fingers seemed stroking its keys. Skins of wild animals were under foot, and before him a large ottoman overhung with something scarlet. At his elbow the undraped figure of a statue stood black and erect outlined with a pencilling of orange light. He groped round for the electric switch, and as he did so, the statue bent down and kissed him.

So, let the curtain descend amidst cries of shame from the audience which pays to witness such plays.

CHAPTER IV

'If Beauty were a mortal thing
That died like laughter, grief, and lust
The poet would not need to sing
If beauty were a mortal thing
It would not wound us with its sting.
We should lie happy in the dust
If beauty were a mortal thing
That died like laughter, grief, and lust.'

The heroes and heroines of modern novels sin, and sin frequently, but always from the highest possible motives. The same cannot be said of Willie. Unlike them, but like so many ordinary people who inhabit earth, he knew quite well that what he did was wrong. And he did it.

Mrs. Bramsbury-Stuart was much more like a heroine. The thought never occurred to her.

To search for reasons is not to find excuses. The reason (so far as Willie is considered) behind that behaviour and course of life which he adopted and continued for a time during the period previous to the breaking out of the Great War, is the reason which lies behind three quarters of all the sins which are committed upon earth – boredom.

To be bored is to be idle. To do the wrong work is to leave unemployed that part of you which is most active. It is to be bored and idle – a state long accepted as one particularly suited to the designs of Satan.

And the reason why boredom is at the back of almost every sin, and is in itself a sin of deepest dye, is that it is a closing of the eyes to God, and all the nobleness of life. Gratitude that sweet child of Huanity is necessarily outcast from it, and with her all the fortifying and heavenly graces. It houses instead a narrow selfishness, and feeds it on lies. Courage only remains, and he weak with a poisonous pride.

Willie was thus fair game for His Majesty. At least four-fifths of his nature was unemployed – and the rest was of little consequence to himself or anyone else.

Men are only good when they are working in their vocation – that is body and soul. All men who makes beautiful things are good – while they are making them. But we make nothing. The greatest manufacturing country in the world makes nothing. So it is unhappy, and no amount of payment seems to be (or is) a just reward for its labour.

The men who built the cathedrals, the men of the guilds – ah, but now we touch politics! Let this only be said – When man is not a maker, he is a destroyer. It is a truth which the world will have to remember before this century is out ...

But there is no doubt that Mrs Bransbury-Stuart found her merman glorious, (as for certain mad hours, he, her). This unaccountable dark lover, whose appearance suggested a strayed gnome, whose humour flashed so gaily and bitterly, was a fascinating contrast to any of his sleek predecessors. So that she actually forgot to provide him with contemporaries!

And to him, she was a sedative. Which of them loved least it would be hard to say; for it would not seem possible to give less love than did he; yet perhaps even then, she was the better off, – giving none.

But love is a queer word which may mean almost anything. To take it at their own valuation – passion was to her an art, but to him only a pastime. Therefore she loved, if you like to put it so, with more of herself. Where he fell (easily enough) into sin, she executed a beautiful and deliberate dive. Women called her 'a bad woman,' men 'a sport,' but she was neither – Simply a highly-sexual and frankly pagan woman, endowed with many generous impulses. Children remembered her with gratitude during the miners' strike – that is something.

As for Willie – Man's passion is possibly smaller than woman's. Certainly it was he who first tired of the liaison. That may be partly accounted for by the fact that this sexual adventure was to him never more than – an adventure. He was hastening to forget life, while she was hastening to remember it. Here was the satisfaction of curiosity, pleasure, risk ... little more. Yet in a certain way he loved her. She had been good to him in Hell...

But slowly, inevitably, it was borne in upon him – through mind and body and spirit – that this life which he was living was Hell.

That dark underground passage into which he had strayed at home shut him off no less effectually from Life than this. He felt the same gasping terror at his throat. He was not living. He was buried alive.

'There is no happiness but the serving of something noble with your heart and strength' – runs his diary at this time. 'A "cause" is lacking to the happiness of millions of people. But where is it?' (This was at the end of the year nineteen thirteen).

And again – 'The senses can divert, but never satisfy – except they are attached to some eternal thing.'

And he concludes – 'Nobleness mucst use us for its own purposes.'

Then – 'What am I doing?' And again – 'What am I doing?'.

But it was not until the early summer of 1914 that he broke away. It happened in this way:–

He had walked all night, soothed with bodily exercise, and that darkness which hid or ennobled the landscape – chimneys turning to star-crowned shadows; mean streets to winding silences; slums mercifully blotted out, and so into country where nothing was discernible but vague outlines of trees and hedges. Over all was the owner of heaven – strange clouds trailing with majesty over the moon, stars seeking their inevitable places.

At morning he had returned to town full of these memories of beauty. Then, seeing life arise sordidly to its sordid tasks 'What in the name of sense is living man doing here?' he cried. 'I will turn my back upon it for ever.' So, meaning to give a month's notice to his employer that morning, he had faced the good-humoured chaff of his landlady, and after breakfasting (and paying his week's bill, since the day was a Saturday) had gone to office, weary but more content at heart than for many a month.

'I must say goodbye to Violet, I suppose,' he had ruminated on the way. And then, when he arrived there he heard that Violet was dead.

It's a bad business about Mrs. Bransbury-Stuart,' said a clerk.

'What?' said Willie startled.

'Haven't you heard? she's shot!'

'Shot!'

'Yes, the old man did it. He'd been drinking a lot, it seems, lately. And then last night they had a quarrel. He accused her of siding with the men who had ruined his pit, and she told him outright that she did, and had used her money, and his, to help their children, and anybody that was starving among them. And he got queer and took a gun and killed her; blew her heard nearly off. Mad, I supp–'.

'Good God!' ...

'Hold up! Arn't you well, Mr. Harvey?' said the repentant man who had told the story callously in the light of certain rumours as to Willie's relations with the dead woman (there are men like that!) and was now thoroughly alarmed at its effect. His victim's face was chalky. His limbs could but just support him.

Then, as he lurched from the room – 'Why must people always pay for their virtues?' Willie cried – and those were the last words they heard him speak. Then and there he left that place of accursed memories.

CHAPTER V

Eric had gone to Oxford to work. He was no longer at a time of life when he could afford to let Time drift by an idly and deliciously as the green-tunneled waters of 'Char' (Charnall) under that dreaming Youth which throngs it each summer day. Had he gone up from school that leisure (and it is not to be despised) might have been his, but now.

Yet Oxford is a sweet mother alike to those who 'fleet the time carelessly as they did in the golden age,' seeking, consciously or not, the noon of pleasant memories, and to those whose preoccupation with graver problems causes them to meet her smile with looks less joyfully insouciant. Her whie lovely towers, sunlit or moonlit, and lovely and vital youth which thronged beneath in 1913 – in 1913! Wherefore Eric always looked upon that year immediately prior to war as one of the happiest of his life; a thing which could be remembered in trenches with longing and with gratitude.

But Willie even in trenches cursed its memory, and would at no time have budged a foot to step back into that same year, if magically the chance had ever been his – as it was not. For death in certain company is better than life in another, and, the soul being sick, there is a terror of mere living which – but this is to digress.

Eric had his difficulties. The course of true love, even for Christ, seldom, if ever, 'runs smooth'. Yet on the side of nobleness enlisted firmly one meets difficulties at pleasant storms, and even disillusion itself carries no terror.

Eric encountered both and, being human, found the latter less tolerable (though disillusion is in fact but a step nearer Truth – that which unmoved abides the ages!).

It is difficult for a grown man to go back to schooldays and learn again the things he could so much more easily have learnt then. Yet the difficulties even of Greek vanished before the knowledge that it was a step towards Christ's badge of service – nay, became a joy. In all his hardships he was (as Willie had said) 'on the road'.

When he stepped off it, or seemed to, was in his disillusions.

There is no doubt that the Varsity that year lost a fine centre forward at soccer, and a fourth wicket bat at cricket who might have saved them against Cambridge. But it was blissfully unconscious of the fact, and so had no cause for tears. College games gave Eric all the recreation he needed for his work. He too was satisfied. He no longer took these things seriously – and had probably never done so. But in talks after matches were over, in the general conversation, in the lectures themselves, he discovered the church of Christ viewed in a light which gave cause for deep reflection, the attitude was general, and (this, the point) was not without reason as a foundation. He took it seriously because he was compelled to.

'You will meet useful people here – the chaps to give you preferment,' was a phrase which apparently explained his very presence amongst these men – nice fellows. It has never entered his head. They said it was a matter of fact. Then he was led to watch other men who were preparing to take 'Holy Orders'. He considered their habitual association with men of position, which could be explained onno other ground – their seeking; their flattery of these people with whom no decent man would exchange 'Good-day'. What answer had he to himself? – to his friends?

He thought. And he replied – 'Then do away with the influence of mere wealth – if necessary with all endowment.' They laughed. 'Then the funny old C. of E. is finished. The chief bulwark of the country against an onslaught of democracy goes down. We must rediscover St Francis!'

'Christianity is the first and the last defence of democracy!', he cried. But without contradicting that statement – which was true – they answered that it was not the question. 'What we are talking about is (what we know) the jolly old C. of E.'

'But does not that Church stand as organised Christianity, both here and the world over?'

'Ask yourself!' they said. And he was friven to carried out the advice – a very disheartening process! (Why disheartening? Reader – ask yourself!).

Again and again he read, pondered, and prayed over, the Sermon on the Mount. Those were Christ's words. He viewed them as no more code of morality, but as of One Who lived – Who was present with all. He prayed to Him.

Quite casually, someone then told him of the reply made by Bernard Shaw to a carpenter who wrote saying he had been 'Converted to Socialism'. 'What shall I do?' he had asked. 'Make yourself the best carpenter in the village' was Shaw's reported reply.

'Then,' said Eric, 'the children of this world verily are wiser than the children of light. What concern is the Church of England and its doings to me? Let me only make myself 'the best carpenter in the village!'. And he worked harder than ever.

Yet joyfully to join an army upholds, and in this trouble he was again and again driven into agreement with a pronouncement of what laughing philosopher of our age – G.K. Chesterton – to the effect that Christianity had not (as many appeared to think) failed in its trial; but that it had been tried, and found difficult, and abandoned – this not only by the people, but by the clergy themselves.

'The R.C.s may, as some think and others deny, hold fast to superstitions' said a scoffing footballer to him one evening, 'but they command this respect, that they hold to the only church which permits a vow of poverty, and actually enforce a celibacy which results in the only effective missionary work in the world.'

'But did Christ?' asked Eric.

'I haven't the least idea, but at all events they give up something to their faith,' was the reply of that very average man, and he was provoked to add – 'The patron Saint of these people is said to be Peter. He was crucified for his God though he trice denied him. Who is yours?'

'I don't think we have anyone but Christ.'

'You have though, if any of us are to believe our ears – Thomas.'

'What do you mean?'

'Only that you may believe just what you like, and just as much of that as you bally well want to. Of course you mustn't do everything,' he concluded slyly.

Eric tried to argue that dogmas were sign-posts to point the way, rather than brick walls to keep people in, but he did not convince even himself. He knew that to take a thing with both hands you must let fall whatever is in them. 'But does that also apply to one's head?' he asked himself – and replied most crushingly, 'that depends on what is inside,' adding 'Yes, your head of all things must be swept clean of fashionable rubbish' ...

As so he turned again to the Sermon on the Mount, and was comforted, but also perplexed. 'Was it true that Christ by that meant the teaching of non-resistance to evil which Tolstoy had expounded?' The war had not then come, but there was sufficient talk of its likelihood (though that had been going on for years) to make the decision of importance to Christians.

'O Lord Jesus,' he prayed, 'I love you and I want to serve you faithfully and truly at any cost, at any price of suffering and endeavour. Then show me how! Let me understand your commands!'

That prayer was answered only by the sudden news of war's proclamation, which fell like a clap of thunder upon millions of ears.

CHAPTER VI

'Had not the fortune of the commonwealth
Come Pallas-like to every Roman thought.'

It happened in the long vacation. Eric was keeping himself fit –
running up body and mind – by work in the hay-fields. Those
Gloucestershire hayfields were in fact his last peace-memory of
England. How fittingly so! At more the continuing corncrake rattle
of the mowing machine began with the first song of the birds, before
sunrise – for grass should be cut with the dew upon it. A scraping
of stone against ringing metal told of scythes being sharpened to
mow the corners and nooks of the meadow and such uneven patches,
banks, and 'grips' as should be found inaccessible to the long and
level blade of the machine pulled round and round in an ever nar-
rowing circle by two horses who never became giddy.

Round and round they went like horses in a dream driven by Sleep
himself in the shape of an ancient and bearded man by name of
Rehoboam. Nodding wise patient faces, went the three together.

The swathed grass was turned and tedded to dry and sweeten in
sun and wind. It was cocked to keep out the dense dew, and, having
ripened to hay, carried to rick yards beyond reach of winter flood
on waggons whose rumble was mixed with song and hoof clatter
as they swayed through quarter of a mile of rutted lane whose leafage was only cleared of hay-whisps when the autumn gales bared all
branches thereabouts.

On August the 5th they were pitching the last loads of that field
called Cornham which was one of the great Severn meadows once
owned by Eric's father (and still by his mother) but now let to a
neighbouring farmer and cider maker – John Helps, one of whose
workmen (being a reservist) had received his papers and departed
mysteriously a day or two before. It was a soldier's place which Eric
had volunteered to take in the hayfield, and the fact revived in his
head all those old arguments about 'non resistance to evil' which

had recently been born in him in his pondering upon the Sermon on the Mount.

Ned Holly – he knew him well – had gone away. By this time who knows but that he was not already in Flanders risking stolidly all he had to keep back the German hordes whose atrocities were filling every newspaper in the land. Holly, that simple country man ... It was queer! For two days Eric had considered it as he kept his place in a rhythmic line of rakers, and now pitching hay to the loaders he was worked to a feverish excitement which caused his fellow work-ers to marvel at such industry, for they could not keep pace with it. The dream-like and regular rhythm, 'without haste, without rest', which is the work of a skilled haymaker, had quickened monstrously to an exhausting display of effort which yet did not tire him – as all prophesied was bound to happen in an hour or two.

'Tolstoy may or may not be right about the message of the Sermon on the Mount, but he is undoubtedly right in saying that every man should each day perform some body-labour,' grunted Eric, heaving up an enormous hay-cock.

'Steady there, maaster Ereich: Quiet does it!' remonstrated a shiny loader. Sweat was dripping like rain from Eric's face, which had a queer look as though the eyes were watching things more real than that hay-field... More real than a Gloucestershire hayfield!

'Ned Holly may now be killed!' he thought. Evening mists turned a sinking sun to the colour of blood. It seemed to Eric like the blood of a guideless man and of his master Christ. 'Ned was not a reli-gious man, but religious or not, the cause was noble for which he risked dear life; perhaps already has laid it down!' Eric balanced up another haycock, forgetting to turn the prongs of his pike inward to the waggon so that it might be slipped off.

'Tother way!' cried down a loader.

Eric twisted his hill of hay till it lay correctly.

'How can a man be noble,' he asked, 'save by taking the path of Gethsemane? Tragedy is the crown set upon all human nobility. It has always been so.'

And again, as he lifted his load of lightness – purging his spirit – 'If this is the war to end war –.'

And again, 'War, barbarous bloody war – I hate it! but for that reason, must I hand over all sacred things to desecration of brutes and bullies?'

The voices of his work-mates uttered England. That old country-man to whom he was pitching hay – badly enough he knew –, was in humour, in patience, something to be kept – as he was. The life he had led was hard but sweet – good. (Why people in towns ever enlisted he never truly knew.) That life must be preserved! ...

And then a soldier entered the field. He walked up against the sun through the last hay-cocks. And knowing him, even in khaki, 'Willie!' cried Eric, and dropped his pike under the horse's hooves.

'Where have you been? We haven't heard from you for a month,' he cried, and kissed him.

'That,' said Willie, dropping a mock salute as he disengaged himself, 'is a long story. I will keep it till we get home to sleep again in the same bedroom. But it will be only once more, for I am now (pointing to his uniform) a "tommy" of His Majesty's Expeditionary Force.'

'It will be more than once that we shall sleep together again,' said Eric, 'though God knows where we may sleep hereafter! But take off your coat off – well, tunic,' he added at Willie's correction, 'and go with a memory of England, and what she is, in your mind – take my pike!'

Willie took it (having greeted the men of his country) and worked for dear life – yet not so unbearably fast as had his brother. And Eric threw himself down on a haycock, and watched. Tears were in his eyes.

The last load was piled. Trampling with song and a jingle of harness the horses brought it home.

'Cover 'un wi' a tarpaulin, and lit un bide!'

Tots of cider were drained, hands shaken, and the brothers walked home together. 'How's Mother?' asked Willie.

'She'll be glad to see you,' said Eric, 'even in that' – pointing to his uniform.

'And I her.'

'She – we – were getting anxious.'

'I was afraid you would be.'

'But where – '.

'I'll tell you later – tonight. I am safe now anyway. The war has saved me!' cried this surprising brother.

They had crossed the home barton and were approaching the farm-house. Familiar sounds, smells and shadows brought tears to Willie's eyes.

'You haven't seen her?' asked Eric.

'No, old Tom Jones (I met him) told me you were working in Cornham, and I came straight there. I was ashamed (why I don't know) to see her ... Afraid ... I didn't know what she would say, or rather what I should say, and how she would look.

'She loves you,' said Eric. 'Let me go on first, and say you've come.' He stepped quickly on, and Willie followed slowly up the mossed garden path between roses and dark dahlia threaded like two seasons upon a twisted line of faint forget-me-not and love-in-the-mist.

Ere either had reached the door, Mrs. Harvey came out carrying something in her hands. She was wearing her bonnet and outdoor cape. She stood on the first of those three steps which are sheltered with trellised jassimine and passion flower. Willie watched her blinking to recognise him. 'Hullo, Mother!' he cried.

'Darling! It is you. I felt it was – only those clothes. My poor eyes wouldn't recognise you. Well, if they make you happy ... You look happy. Kiss me! Now take care' (as Willie embraced her), 'these eggs are for a poor dying woman'

'What can a dying woman want with eggs, darling?'

'Ah, poor soul, she can't die.'

'Then it's Nanny Rivers!' cried he, thinking of that wrinkled face and rounded hoop-like body which had been the terror of children and even of grown-ups who were timid or dealt in superstition. 'The witch!' they cried from afar. She, ten years ago, had taken to her bed to die at seventy years – the allotted span. But she could not. People said that neither the devil or the angels would have her. She had lived an evil youth (the more appalling since none could remember it!) and every midnight a ghostly hand put back the fingers of the clock – a tall, black and grim 'grandfather' into which a child might creep, or be shut away – so that it never chimed, but told always the same day, standing at the foot of her bed, like an evil presence.

'The witch,' laughed Willie.

'Only a poor, old woman – as I shall be some day – with a mind that rambles back and back.'

'Don't talk so, dearest!'

'Come with me then!' Willie took from her hand the basked of eggs! 'It was cruel of you not to write,' she began, 'but –'.

'I know that,' said Willie, but –'. (Eric had gone forward to the house.)

'There is no need of 'buts', darling,' said Mrs. Harvey to her son as they walked together, 'we love one another ... Only I am very sorry that you have been unhappy, and I am glad that you are happy again, even if that means that I must lose you.' Willie choked.

'I suppose I must lose Eric, too?' she enquired. Willie nodded, and by this time they had arrived at the cottage. They tapped on the door.

'Come in, then!' called a voice in something between a welcome and a curse. The old yellow face seemed to brighten a little on recognition of her visitors. A frightened little girl who had come in to look after the old woman arose and offered her chair to Mrs. Harvey. Willie remained standing. The propped-up, bedridden woman gazed piercingly upon both on them. 'Bible,' she said. Recognition vanished from her eyes.

'Eric usually comes with me and reads bits out of the Gospels' whispered her mother to Willie. She put a bottle of brandy and the eggs on a shelf in a corner of the room, and sat down.

'She says she have got noises in her head,' said the little girl.

'Such drummerdery noises!' cried a sepulchral voice from the bed. Those words were all she said during their visit save for a disconnected word or two muttered to herself. 'Summer,' and 'Summer' again; and then in a voice of fear, 'water-floods!' and 'fires! fires!'.

'Let not your heart be troubled' … Willie heard his mother reading … 'In my Father's house are many mansions' … and again, 'I am the way, the truth, and the life.' The tall clock ticked on at the bed-foot.

Then they said goodbye to the frightened little girl, and departed.

'So I must lose both my babies. When do you go?'

'Not out of England for a good long time I expect,' answered Willie, 'but my leave is up tomorrow – Sunday evening.'

'So soon.'

'I think Eric means to come with me.'

'I am not surprised. He is a good boy. I have heard him in the room next praying loud like Christ in the garden these last three nights. This terrible war is on his mind heavy and heavy. He couldn't tell what was the right thing to do. Now he will be less unhappy – with a decision come to.'

'You are much more happy than you have been for a year,' she said as they re-entered the garden.

'That is true, Mother.'

'I can see it in your face, and I am glad; but the misery that can be made glad by such a thing as war frightens me more than any death dangering the body of my son' – she cried clasping his hand – 'my first little son!'

Now she was weeping.

'Dear, dear Mother – don't cry! I am happy – in everything but the thought of leaving you here alone. I have leapt into chances to live as a man should, to risk life finely for all I love: instead of living like a beetle … a snake … a crawling poison'

'Dearest, don't! how unhappy you must have been!'

'Yes, I am sick,' he cried, 'of bread at the world's price. I will eat it at God's price – joyfully – though I eat nothing after. The hope fills me with glorious happiness.'

'Then, if my sons are happy, I have no excuse to be unhappy. They are all I have left, God save them!' spoke his mother as they entered the house.

CHAPTER VII

Of his life at Eccleton Willie would not speak, but after supper had been cleared away, he sketched, with the help of tobacco, what kind of life had befallen him since his hurried departure from it.

'For a long time existence generally, and all that law business in particular, had been just a swarm of flies round my head,' he began by way of explaining his flight. 'I thought that as time went on I should be able to shut a door in my brain when I left office, and then live – I mean write. But I never could. For nine months I wrote nothing – nothing. My leisure was full of that same buzz. And yet,' he concluded, 'to produce lovely things is the only real life ...' Eric nodded. 'Not only that, but the old poems, and stories, the plays, I had poured my heart into when that was living, came back one after another, so that I ceased to send them out any more. And on the top of all this something else happened – very dreadful, though not a personal tragedy. A woman was murdered ... Life that was already sordid turned to living death in such a place, and I left it without saying a word to you or to anybody. I just walked out of the office, and out of the town. Nobody there knew my home address. You thought I was in Eccleton. They thought I was at home, and anyway didn't care where I was, having in hand about six weeks salary, and being able easily to fill my place.

'It was a bright summer's morning. On my way I remember meeting a pimpled parson (no offence, old man!) and three or four young men. They were weakly hideous, but he was like a gargoyle – only a gargoyle is funny. I got out of the town – south west as it happened – but going anywhere away from it. Then I passed a blind man singing 'Lead kindly light,' a wanderer like myself, but he tried to steal the bit of money I had, in the lodging-house where we slept, and I went on next morning, marching anywhere, but towards Gloucestershire as it turned out. Next day I walked out into a grey, strange world. How still: how vigorous yet spell-bound! The summer meadows lay in white mist which magnified the great cart horses as they limped slowly round tearing off grey-green grass.

'I breakfasted on bread and cheese in a wood by the roadside. It was old and deserted by the birds, though a few rook nests hung in its high trees. Soon a light appeared in the east. The sky intensified its blue. As I left the wood veins of gold ran intersecting upon heaven in a sort of steady lightning. It was light rimming the clouds fantastically shaped to eastward. I turned my back upon that and marched. My shadow leapt before me a hundred yards on the white road. The odour of morning-earth uprose.For the first time that year I felt myself a living man. Remembering my past life, I said to old grandpa who was present in that earth-smell: "Grandfather, I have sinned against heaven and before thee and am worthy no more to be called grandson! I (and many) never believed that you were dead for three weeks – never understood that it was possible. Yet I have been sad for a year and more. Blackbirds fluted in orchards, and I did not hear. Apple bloom was a dazzle of white, and I did not see. So my brain became Severn and mud taking no hard impression of things lovely; and life something dirtier than that: It was not to live. I grant that I have been dead and have risen again, even as you did!"

Eric and his mother chuckled. Willie continued: 'I walked on. I came to a village, and sitting there on a doorstep were two mites in blue overalls (like Eric and I used to wear) feeding a dog with a basin of bread and milk. I was talking to them about ducks and hens – how a hen had long horny toes, but a duck 'flat skin between his scratchers,' when out came their father, an interesting fellow (mason by profession), who told me that his father, an old man of eighty, was dying upstairs. And nothing would please him but that he should make a will, wherefore he (the son) was for finding a lawyer to do it – though since he as only son would naturally inherit everything the old man had to leave him there seemed no sense in it. So I told him that, as fate willed it, he need go no further, since I was a solicitor – which for a time he was reluctant to believe, but was at last satisfied, or possibly thought it didn't matter.

So I went upstairs into a room which smelt of dead man, and at the dictation of a poor hawk-nosed corpse with a white billy goat beard, wrote:–

'This is the last will and testament of me, Joseph Mitchel, labourer, of Stars Lane in the village of Something in the County of Warwick' (I believe) 'whereby I give and bequeath all real and personal estate whatsoever whereof I at the time of my death do stand possessed to Henry Howard Mitchel, my son,'

It was signed by me and a neighbour 'in the presence of one another both being present at the same time' after we had duly witnessed the cross made by the now satisfied testator on the bland day of blank (July, it was, of course) in the year 1914.

And after that I walked on, leaving my friends the more convinced that I was no lawyer since I would accept no fee. 'Who washes God?' was a last question put to me by the smaller of these two children before I left, and pondering the correct answer to that I went my way, glad to have been a service to old age if not to babyhood.

I slept that night in a shed. (Don't turn up your noses, and look sympathetic!) It was a sight better than the lodging house. Little mice rustled in the straw. The wind sighed hush! hush! over my head. I was lying soft, and cleanly – and alone. A dog poked his wet nose into my face in the morning, but neither I nor he, was afraid. "There is no fear in straw, for clean and perfect straw casteth out fear."

'Don't quote sacred things profanely, dearest,' expostulated his mother.

'All right, darling,' said Will, 'we are agreed – only it's all the same thing. To sleep under stars and clean straw is holy.

And the next day, since my money was getting low, I worked for a farmer in the hay-field, and also the next day after that. Haymaking had just started in that part.

I should have stayed longer than I did at that farm (I did a week there as it was!) Therefore I moved on. She was a hefty woman of thirty-five who brought supper to me in the barn where I slept, and washed and ironed my collar. She's got it now.

In the next village I bought a jolly scarf much more comfortable to wear. True comfort is obtained only by a social descent – in summer.

And so is luxury – the fine luxury of letting your body rest after hard open-air labour.

Tramping on, I had a lovely bathe unseen and cool in the gloom of a tunnel which conveyed a clean little brook under the road. There was dusty traffic rumbling but a few yards over my head, and – "how short a distance off the common highway lies fairyland!" thought I, lying in little green forest of moss as slanting light seemed lazily to open and close its eyes, gilding those ripples which reflected its ringed blinking upon the tunnel's roof.

It was in Worcestershire, near Pershore, that I first heard tidings of the war. 'And wot be we gwine ter do when them bloody allies do come to rape and ruin us all?' enquired rhetorically an ancient stone breaker of very unseductive appearance, having a mouth like a kipper's, and a face of divine discontent.

At Gloucester barracks I enlisted because I discovered that soldiers did not wear stiff collars in war time – and for other reasons. But before that, a queer thing had happened to me. Within Gloucestershire, but on the borders by Broadway whither I had come wandering I fell in with a camp of gypsies. And who – whom – do you think they were? They very same people that we, Eric and I, met in the Forest of Dean a year ago: the same man who had shown us Christ a-weeping: the same lovely girl who told us fortunes: the same three scraggy dogs: the same others of 'em!'

'Meeting them again seems to have impressed you,' said Mrs Harvey.

'It did. It did impress me, and it does still impress me,' replied Will. 'You see, I lived with them for several days. They insisted on giving me hospitality – but that was not the most impressive thing.'

'What then?'

'I don't think I can tell you. Well, to begin with I got to that part thinking. Casual work and not much food but chiefly (since I have actually suffered) a mood of reflection caused it. I remembered that these nights were comparatively warm – how in dying Kingsley, a good Christian, a friend of poor people thanked God for the frost on his window. And then I thought of the people who were outside: who could only shudder with the cold wind, and the vision of some bleak white workhouse, or farms with dogs savagely barking near shiny ricks and friendly barns. I saw the road stretching endlessly, and no courage to walk it.

"Age comes," I said, "and then comfort – mere comfort – tells a fairy tale." I saw old men sitting over fire dreaming their dreams. "And what have old men left?" I asked, pondering on such things as poverty, and old age, and December, on a warm moonlighted night of July.

Spreading a yellower sheet on yellow moonlight a motor rushed callously by me on the road. It offended me in an unreasonable way. I didn't want another car to do that. I got over a wall and into meadows. The clock in some distant steeple had just rung nine faint airy hour-strokes. Time was made precious and audible. The wet meadows lay silver in moonlight. Yet their lovely silver was tarnished when the broad stream which streaked a hollow appeared suddenly as I turned the corner of a wood, and foreboding thoughts which had already melted in those meadows turned suddenly to a startled delight, when as naturally as nymph from shade stole silently out a naked girl.

No thought or image of lust kept me there silent ... watching, as she stood a moment bright upon the brink and then dived. It was sheer loveliness. The lamp-lit artifices of sensuality were in another world. Flakes of cool fire flicked from her limbs as she swam. When she had reached mid-stream I turned, walking I knew not where, but with that image burning like a naked loveliness in my brain – the silver image of one moment!

I in the open night which was my bedroom till morning did not sleep but made a poem which I wrote down at sunrise.

'Flower-like and shy
You stand, sweet mortal, at the river's brim:
With what unconscious grace
Your limbs to some strange law surrendering
Which lifts you clear of our humanity.

Nor would I sacrifice
Your breathing, warmth, and all the strange romance
Of living to a moment. Ere you break
The greater thing than you, I would my eyes
Were basilisk to turn you into stone.
So should you be the world's inheritance ...'

'But what has this to do with the gypsies?' asked Eric and Mrs. Harvey together.

'It was she,' whispered Willie. 'I found their fire next morning, and heard where she had been. She told me of the place – little thinking that I had seen it – and her, the night before. But that was the reason I did not dare go bathe there myself. I kept a memory instead. I shall always keep it. It was sacred beauty and I shall die with it in me ...

I lived with those people for three days and I walked with her in the woods gathering sticks and I don't now what. And we talked ... I remember her saying that sheep were "that foolish it seemed a shame. Their little brains just tell them to eat and drink and lie down.

Then they are driven off and killed and eaten. But rooks" (she thought) "must have a lot of brain in a little head, with their houses thick as the houses in cities all without names or numbers, and they flying miles every night to find each one his own." She liked all wild things especially the birds: them she would never kill, though she considered all animals, especially the rabbits and hedgehogs, meant for food.

She said a lot that I have forgotten for the time, though I don't forget any of it in reality. But she said a very strange thing just before we parted – that I should go over the sea, and that we should meet again there! And that (he added) was another reason why I enlisted.'

'You are in love with that gypsy girl,' said Mrs. Harvey.

Willie shook his head. 'I remember her as a strange beauty – impersonally, no more ...'

'I forget her' he said, gazing at the fire, 'and then blue smoke brings her vividly before me with her dark golden-brown beauty and her blowing dress ... or sometimes moonlight ...' He shivered.

It was a different shiver from that which had caused Mrs. Bransbury-Stuart to smile.

Well, love means many things to many people.

'and so,' he went on (puffing smoke at the ceiling) 'and so I left those people, and came back through Winchcomb and Gloucester, and – here I am.'

'No one was ever more welcome, dearest,' said his mother, and then sighed.

Eric also was thinking of the parting.

'We must eat Holy Communion all three together tomorrow,' he said. 'Let's go to bed now.'

PART V

'THE LINE'

CHAPTER I

'They drills us, and marches us about (marches was not the word, but it will do!) and we goes to Colchester for firing, and gets so many blinkin' "bulls" that the brigadier 'as to put 'is 'and into 'is pocket ant stand footballs to every platoon, and then they sends us back 'ere to dig our way through to Aus-bloody-stralia!'

'Say that again old man, will you?' requested Willie with a smile as he deposited another shovelful of earth upon the parados of the half-dug trench in which they stood.

'What's the matter with Australia without the blood?' asked Eric, laughing.

'Well mate, I should say that it would be kind of anaemic' was the unanswerable retort.

'Phreee!' echoed a whistle. They 'fell in' to march back to billets, to the tune of mouth organs, and songs 'not nice'. Another day, typical of all, was done. In an hour's time the regiment would be off duty: free to play cards, drink beer, go 'skirt-hunting', or write letters, as mood and the provost-marshall permitted.

Ninety per cent of the men were 'old hands' of the county territorial unit, who had volunteered to go to the front: the rest, replacing those who found reasons for not so volunteering, and bringing the regiment up to 'strength', were recruits. In this latter category were Willie and Eric, the whole of the county Rugby fifteen, half the Gloucester rowing club, and a score of other boys of various class, occupation, and kind.

The common factor was simply that they were all Gloucestershire soldiers, and the accent must be placed upon the county, since to none was soldiering a profession. They were patriotic in a sense of the word unknown to cosmopolitan 'Empire builders'.

'I always knew the old county was good, but where on earth did this assortment of nobility arrive from, even within it?' asked Willie after his first week. Eric's explanation was logical and orthodox to Christians. They were God's children.

'But the parsons know nothing of 'em' retorted his brother. 'They are only shocked by their swear words!'

'I am talking of Christ', replied Eric with significance.

'Meaning – ?'

'That 'The Great War' is a chance to wake up, and substitute brothers for "dearly beloved brethren" . It isn't easy' he added. 'We've been bred to mix with people, but this is something staggering in the way of revelation even to farmbred folks. Consider what a difference of manners means to most folks!'

'Well, it didn't to the disciples' was a natural retort. 'Not that I'm arguing for the self-vanity of a proletariat that imagines it can't be improved, and won't learn' or the damnable heresy "vox populi, vox Dei". But these chaps are the salt of the earth. And they are outside the pale!'

'The war will change that' said Eric. 'That is my belief: that is what I am fighting for.'

('How unfortunate' sighs the Ironic Muse, 'that he died for his belief!')

'Good lad!' said Willie; 'may we live to see it! It is a pity that every parson is not encouraged or forced to join the ranks of the new army instead of forbidden to do it. A university is nothing to this.' Eric agreed.

'I often wonder why I am going to fight' said Willie. 'It is not because I am out of work. I could get that, and more than a bob a day, easily enough; and I know that none of the reasons allegedly in newspapers will account for it in my or three parts of the other chaps here. In us abstract principle may count something, but it is not much, and when we come to concrete things what have we got to defend? Would we die – (to give your life is the last test of any man's conviction) – would we die for any of these catch phrases? Yet we are ready – all here – to die for something ...'

'Since it is not the kingdom of Earth, it may be the Kingdom of heaven' suggested Eric.

'I think it is Gloucestershire – and what she means ... We would rather die for that, than live for Eccleton – and what it means.'

'Yet Eccleton is probably raising forces' said Eric.

'No doubt – and that is what I don't understand, unless it is just – better the hell you don't know, than the hell you do!'

Eric laughed. 'That's a good misquotation' said he.

'Well, let's leave it at 'Something'. That has always been your motto in life, old man, hasn't it?'

'Let what we die for be some blessed abstract beauty – not some concrete floor', spoke Willie epigrammatically, but knowing well that there was no such thing as abstract beauty. 'Call it Gloucestershire – though it is rather some mixture of adventure and beauty bred out of her!'

'It is love of home' said his brother, 'yet that home is but glimpsed in Gloucestershire. It is not of the earth, though mirrored in it, to you and such poets.'

That was true. To the hill of Flanders ran two different roads. But they led through it, and on to the same destination. Call it Home!

Now if this book has a hero (or heroes) the argument must stand for that. And remember that it was typical (though some would deny it) of every other regiment raised in England in the early part of the war. It is beyond the scope of story-telling to trace the lives of a thousand soldiers, and fortunate that (as fruit of an earlier combined effort between writer and reader) we now stand intimately with the lives of two who must exist not merely as separate personalities but also as symbols of the rest – of all who took one of two roads leading to Flanders.

It is the symbolic likeness, not the personal idiosyncrasy, which is important. But the latter had to be drawn, because lacking it the figures would seem such unconvincing puppets that the reader could not imagine them representing anything. Therefore attention has so been carefully focussed upon two people, and this was an artistic necessity. It is still a necessity since the story must to told. But that story would not need to be told and never should be told, did not those two people stand for more than themselves: for England: for the dead.

Willie and Eric differing superficially from one another (as from their fellows) must be a million men. They must stand as the two main types of volunteer in the year 1914. The fact that they did volunteer makes analysis curious and of interest. A conscientious objector is psychologically plain sailing:– besides he is alive, you may ask him! The movie of a conscript in joining up needs to subtility of analysis. But these thousands ...!

There was Headler, a surveyor, Gurney, an art student, Ridley, a bank clerk, Stinchcombe, a labour, Higham, a lawyer's clerk, Willie, a lawyer, Wilteley, a miner of the Dean Forest, Walker, God knows what! Eric, an embryo parson, Meadows, a farm hand, Knight, a schoolmaster and an old 'blue', Brookfield, a poacher, Whatley – why go on? There were:

'As many tempers, moods, and minds
As leaves are on a tree.'

And that simile is the more perfect because of the single life which they lived together, and the common root that nourished it.

Youth was not the name of that root. Ages varied from 16 to 40. But all these men were of the county.

When (no doubt under press of casualties) the War Office recruited indiscriminately to any regiment, it offended something deeper than mere preference. There is more than safety in numbers. There is joy. But that joy is known best to those who are in company with their countrymen. It makes the difference there is between 'a team', and 'eleven players'.

This must be set down to assure readers of something which is nowadays in danger of being forgotten in a very admirable hatred of war and whose forgetting must cause misunderstanding of certain men with whom the story is concerned. (That is an artist's only excuse for digression.)

Truth will permit no question of these men going sorrowfully to war, driven like sheep to slaughter. That is a false modern idea.

I say, and I know, that there was joy in those days even in filthy death. John Meadows' jokes gave courage and bravery in the worst trenches. Ray Knight's gay and gallant soul shone like fire upon the coldest night. Some cannot understand this. But they have not lived with these men.

Believe, and go on with the tale! Or believe not, and shut the book!

Such men were joyful in one another's company. Circumstances could not vanquish that joy. It illuminated billets here,and barns in Flanders. It did not fall in the filthiest trench, with grunted oaths for common speech – oaths which have been seized upon by smart journalists to prove (in prose or poetry) the obsession of things which were never in their hearts – hate and despair. One can show war as the horror it is, without telling lies about soldiers. Soldiers were far the least comfortable, but far the most happy of England's population during the war.

Not that they were all saints or even pleasant fellows. There were in this regiment characters quite as despicable as any civilian. The joy of a wide unique comradeship, which was the joy of those days, was sometimes dissipated. There were private soldiers whose chief passion was to obtain stripes. There were dignified lance-corporals.

It happened soon after that day's trench digging mentioned that the Adjutant's groom received (via the Adjutant's horse) a rumour which turned out true! The regiment departed in a night. Its destination was not as stated. It was ... halt! Before this departure, something else happened. This must be related since it affects the story of Willie and Eric, and reveals them adequate representatives of men who enlisted (a) in a spirit of adventure, and (b) for conscious principle – which two types (speaking generally) composed the regiment, though each was inclined to overlap and blend as it appreciated the other's secret.

A telegram came. Mrs. Harvey was, it turned out, ill, and moreover in sudden financial straits owing to the failure of a bank. She had concealed the former circumstance, but a relative revealed it simultaneously with the latter, saying that application to Authority had resulted in the decision that one of the two boys should be released from military service to attend to affairs. It was suggested that Willie, as the lawyer, should come home.

'Good lord! But why me?' asked Willie. 'You have been a bank clerk. You understand business. And you hate it less than I hate it. Why should I go?'

'Well, one of us has got to go.'

'Then you go. How can I leave these chaps on the eve of going to the front? What will they think of me?'

'The same as they will think of me if I go' said Eric, 'and that will be nothing bad, I hope. But anyway it's a poor soldier who won't do his duty because of public opinion. I'll go if you prefer it. I can join up again later.'

'You are a brick, I am just a moral coward' cried Willie. 'But it isn't only that. For you will do the work just as well. And, though cowardice is at the bottom of my wish, it isn't a fear of opinion. It's deeper. After the way life treated me – the muck I made of it. (But you don't know all that.) I found peace in war, and home, among these men. It is leaving those things that frightens me. I dread going back to the old life – to anything that reminds me of it.'

'I understand', said his brother. 'Shake hands, old man. It's settled.'

So Eric went home a few days before the battalion crossed to Flanders. His comrades were sorry – they loved his kind quiet says. But comment was drowned in the excitement of the move, and was always characteristically understanding of the circumstances, save in one instance.

They had fallen in for roll call on the eve of departure. Willie having answered his name, Eric's was called by chance – the roll being an old one. There was no answer. 'Oh, he's left us, hasn't he?' said the sergeant, correcting the list.

'The only jibber', answered a newly-made corporal, by no means famed for his anxiety to see active service.

'Say that again, and stripes or none I'll knock your teeth down your throat!' cried Willie, flaming.

'Silence!' shouted the sergeant. 'Kindly apologise for that remark, Corporal.'

'I didn't mean –' shamefacedly began the N.C.O.

'That'll do then! And you, Private Harvey, remember that you are on parade.'

Willie resumed a rigid position in the ranks, but murder was in his heart as they moved off – it was not directed against a foreign enemy.

CHAPTER II

Now where is Clemmy to watch these hundreds of little boys return exhausted and smarting from her nettles?

Let her face loom above the Flanders battle fields: let her smile beam cynically upon those barns where rest the weary men! Smile back at her, brothers: call her endearingly our civilisation!

'Dear Mother: (wrote Willie) I am so very glad to hear, from Eric, that you are getting better and that the operation was a success. We are back from an eight day spell of trenches in a lovely barn dangerously lighted with candles stuck in the rings of bayonets. The bayonet makes an admirable hold for shaved candles when stuck perpendicularly in the earth. That is the only use we have made of it so far – except to toast impaled bacon upon the point!

There seems no sign of move on either side at present. It is a rotten business. Not that I long for slaughter like a true patriot, but because the war can't end in this way. Our nice sergeant was 'sniped' the day before we came out. Shells killed four others, but otherwise the platoon is as it was – a little dirtier, and a little more serious – that's all.

Everyone remains cheery; to-night (and since 'wang rouge' and clean straw are available) almost hilarious. Discomforts are soon forgot; and sorrows (we feel) not worth brooding upon. May we die as clearly as those, and as quickly! My dread is a bullet in the stomach. That is the reason I carry morphia – enough to end the tournament. God, I feel, will forgive the deed; and you, and Eric – so parsons may go hand – all except our chaplain, who is as likely as not to have to do the same himself!

He has taken a dug-out which he calls 'The Vicarage', and is the hero of a tale wrongly reported of someone else. A party of the Bucks marching in on relief passed the shelter. 'Look', said one, 'there's a blasted vicarage!'

'And here's the blasted vicar!' answered H, sticking out his head.

He has started a trench paper, of which I enclose a copy. Sandwiched between the casualties and some delicious regimental scandals are a couple of poems by me. It is queer to get published after all my efforts. What pleases me is that the chaps like 'em. Perhaps this is the only public I shall ever have. But it is a good one. A delightfully left-handed compliment was paid me to-night. "I can't read Shakespeare", remarked one of the fellows, 'but I'm damned if I didn't read every word of your thing called "In Flanders".' That's good, isn't it? But listen: "You ought to be ashamed of yourself", he added. 'It made me homesick. It's bloody!'

Dearest, if that's not fame, what is?

Now darling, I am happy and unhurt, so don't worry. But the war won't end yet. If it were to, it would be no use. I am not being pessimistic, but only telling the truth. Eric will be wanted, I'm afraid – though he isn't! He will fiNd rather more comforts at the front than he expects (for like myself he expected none) and as much happiness as true fellowship can give. I am – though nearly smothered in kind ladies' mufflers –

Ever your loving son.'

Things continued for a time much as outlined in Willie's letter. Both armies were marking time: making visits to the front line: losing a few men in the period: returning to billets after eight or ten days to bandy ancient jests in estaminets with the R.E.'s, who directed their fatigues, and A.S.C. men whom they accused of eating strawberry jam all day, and being paid six times as much as front line men, because it was skilled work.

In every army throughout the world the maximum of danger means the minimum of pay, and is cause of such good-humoured chaff. Perhaps the most that can be said for this system is that it provides a standard 'grouse' which is dear as gold to the hearts of infantrymen – even when that gold can purchase but watery beer.

With the end of open order fighting, and those almost superhuman marches on cobbled roads which caused wearied men to conjure up visions of invisible things, a different spirit had settled upon our now entrenched armies. The sense of active crusade had gone, and was succeeded by that of a dogged endurance which coupled itself in the English character to a kind of humour incomprehensible to the rest of the world. This had not (in 1915) turned to the hopeless anger and weariness which possibly manifested itself in later stages.

Bairnsfather had succeeded Rupert Brooke, but Siegfried Sasson had not arrived.

Yet it would be wrong to think that the warfare of that year could from any angle be regarded in the light of a review entitled 'The Better 'Ole'. Setting aside such small matters as Nurse Cavell, the ordinary trench warfare provided little in the way of comedy, though something of grim farce – in retrospect.

A nightmare atmosphere overhung, even in daytime, that Flanders countryside; and darkness only deepened it into horrible reality.

With nightfall, and the snaky rising of Verey lights along irregularly designed trenches, a sense of all dreadful possibilities entered the mind. And these possibilities were inclined to realise.

Agonised men lay helplessly lingering out existence in No-man's-land. Their bodies were brought in by comrades the following night, or left to rot where they lay. Iron torn like brown paper cut living men in half who joked with their friends a minute before. Their blood poured into the ground like wine from a broken bottle. Massed suffering was undoubtedly greater at a later date: individual suffering never so.

Willie volunteered for all night patrols. That was better than standing in a trench to curse the stars that would never go out. That was his nature. He could never wait. Success, danger, glory, death itself, must come quickly. Life missed a glorious opportunity in not condemning him to die lingering through one of those horror-filled nights of his own choosing.

As a matter of fact all he got was a decoration. That was ironic enough, for he had on many occasions gone through similar experience – tasted the same emotions – without thanks. But this time it was a case of one oF two rival patrols being wiped out. And fortune favoured the British.

It placed at the critical moment the Germans against a sky line. It concealed in grass those whom they hunted. With cinema-like haste and inconsequence the scene flashed into sight, twinkled, and vanished, amid groans and excited cries. It might never have happened only that the horrible bodies were brought in three days later to convince the patrollers themselves.

Then the mind could reconstruct the affair. Darkness – a snaky wriggle over the parapet – our wire – suppressed oaths – no-man's-land – whispers – tussocky grass that turned to figures, and back to grass: advance of creeping men keeping touch as best they could over uneven ground; falling flat into filth or water as floating stars lifted from the German lines and drifted slowly down upon them – whispers – sighing wind – more whispers – Germans! – silence broken only by the rattle of machine guns – suspense broken by nothing: peering figures as anxious as they but against the sky line – fire – rapid fire! – a dreadful shriek from one whose belt buckle with its text 'Gott mit uns' had been driven through the stomach – a rush with bayonets – shouts – wriggles – groans – grunts – indiscriminate fire from both trenches – crawling on the belly: excited whispers – challenges – shots from British lines – 'Let us in, you bloody fools!' Cries of recognition – falls into a friendly trench – congratulations then rum – short report – sleep – forgetfulness – and three weeks later, with the battalion in another part of the line, this letter from Willie to end the chapter:

'Dearest: I am expecting leave. What joy to see you and Eric and England again! It is five months since I saw either – and how dear they all seem! I scarcely believed that they existed. That is the curse (and comfort) of this life. It draws you into its atmosphere. You fill sand bags and take risks mechanically, and the very reasons why, are as remote as things which never existed. Not that you are forgotten. Only you seem too good to be true. Memory of you is an act of faith. You exist as Heaven does. Perhaps that is the greatest of all realities. Yet a man expects death before he expects to see it. It is so with you, and Eric, and those English meadows smoking with September.

At risk of being censored I will say that we are now far from Plug Street wood and its amazing nightingales that used to sing above the unnatural thunder of guns: and have marched many a night through silent cobbled towns whose houses gazed blankly upon our commotion (they had seen this before) and then with aching feet, too weary even to sing, yet finding joy in the after memory, unwound the length of lonely roads flanked always with star-crowned poplars, and slept as upon down in barns and open fields. What snores: what curses: what singing: those barns have heard!

And now we are in Picardy trenches opposite another wood. I will say no more. I am lousy, and so is everybody from the Colonel down ...

But I have got (if it please you) a minor sort of decoration to show when I come home, and (which pleases me at all events) some lines on Gonnehun, that rose in our desert of marching – a tiny village enclosing the most gracious little farm imaginable out of England, and the kindest people, and the ripest cherries, and the prettiest little dark-eyed children.

The war goes on in a kind of bloody stupor. Nobody can even guess when it may end. But how, we do not doubt. Meanwhile for a few fortunate people there is leaving pending, and waking up at home in bed, and sweet birds to whistle instead of shells, and mothers, and brothers, and all unbelievable things.

Till then, with best love, I remain your invisible son,

Willie

P.S.

I am sorry to say dear old Stinchcombe has died in hospital. We hoped that he was for Blighty, and his mother, but – the news has just come. Possibly you have heard already. His mother will certainly. Go and see her if you can, and say – well, you know best what to say. There is not much, is there? Only all of us loved him.

CHAPTER III

While this letter was being penned, Mrs. Harvey and Eric sat talking together. Financial affairs had come out better than were expected. Money had been lost, but the land (let off) remained, and that had appreciated in value and so brought better rents. Moreover that which the doctors had feared to be cancer had proved something which surgeons could remove, and the patient had made good recovery. She was an older and greyer woman than Willie knew her, but filled with the same courage.

Probably Eric had aged more than she. It was not a sweet life to any other than those engaged heart and soul in the making of money during 1915, but to a man cut off from the fine men with whom he had enlisted, and misunderstood by those who willingly remained at home, it was a thing which only conviction of righteousness could make tolerable.

Eric had that solace. But he was unhappy.

'Mother', he said, as the log fire crackled in purple spurts and poured a golden torrent up over the chimney soot, 'dear, you are well again, and things are settled as satisfactorily as they can be. I ought ...'

'I know what you are going to say – '

'I ought to join up again.'

'Very well, darling.'

So the talk ended. and a week later Eric departed, entering the old regiment's reserve battalion with a view of joining this brother as soon as possible.

And a week after that, Mrs. Harvey, sitting alone by the same hearth, arose and went to the door in answer to a knock, and peering out upon a dirty grinning apparition in khaki, cried 'Will! It is my dear old Willie!' And the apparition kissed her.

Then, 'Where is Eric?' he enquired. And Mrs. Harvey told him.

'What a shame we shouldn't be able to spend this leave together. Oh well, there are us two, anyway! Thank God for that!'

'Thank God for that, my dear.'

Willie dumped his pack in the hall. He hung up his great coat on a peg, and stood his rifle in the umbrella stand.

'What baggy unsightly trousers they have given you, dearest!'

Willie unbuttoned his tunic and fumbled laughing all the time with his back turned. 'The old soldier always gets baggy trousers if he can, Mother!'

'Why?'

'They fit so nicely over the puttees, and they are so – well baggy, that you can bring home things like this.; And with that he produced from one leg the nose cap of a shell, and from the other a bottle of champagne!

'Good gracious! But did you carry those things all the way from France?' asked the astonished woman.

'Every step,' replied the soldier. 'One isn't supposed to, of course, but no one searches one's trousers.'

'But couldn't you have got the wine at any rate in this country?' enquired Mrs. Harvey, laughing.

'Perhaps, but my experience is against it. I didn't go to a wine merchant's, but they told me in London that the private bar of an Inn was no place for the country's defenders. As a matter of fact I had entered by mistake (for I prefer the public room) and only wanted a glass of beer. But that's the spirit … I told them most of what I wanted to say before I left,' he added dryly.

'I agree with it all, but you need not repeat it, dear.'

'You have read Tristram Shandy, Mother –'

'Our troops swore terribly in Flanders,' she answered. 'And there is sometimes excuse for a little of it over here. It was a shame.'

'Oh, that's of no consequence. I could have got all and more than I wanted at other places,' said Willie. 'This bottle was what the Colonel gave me (he gave us one each when we picked up our D.C.M.'s.), and I wanted to drink it at home with you and Eric – that's all.'

'I will store it away for your son' said Mrs Harvey, 'and get another for you now from the cellar.'

'Don't replace it except with Minsterworth cider – dear optimist! (A wonderful chance we soldiers will have of getting sons!') And then, his bitterness changing at her look, 'To come home is a sufficient intoxication for me, or rather (since that's hardly the point)

I don't feel like drinking. I wanted poor old Eric to pledge us good fortune – you and he and I, all together.'

'Who but God knows good fortune when he sees it: but may both my dear sons find that!' said Mrs Harvey, taking the bottle from his hands. 'Now you are going to have a hot bath, and Dorothy (you must see her first) and I will lay supper for you by the time you have finished. She was so good through all our anxiety and my illness. Most servants have gone away into munition factories now. They can earn so much more money. Her sister has gone into one. But Dorothy refused. I thought she might like to. She is a strong girl and could stand it. Besides, I had promised her a rise in wages and couldn't manage it after all, because of –'

'How did things pan out?' interrupted Willie.

'Better than we had hoped, thanks to Eric's wisdom. A little was saved out of that money. We must rely almost entirely on the land now, but that brings in more. My actual income is only a little below what it was – £250 a year. But everything has increased in price ...'

'And will, I'm afraid' prophesied her son, with greater truth than he knew. 'But where's Dorothy?' I must give her a souvenir, and my gratitude.'

He tramped off to the kitchen, where he deposited a much prized German forage cap, some French buttons, an English half-crown, and a gaudily-woven card bearing in silk the flags of the Allies. It was the latter which Dorothy really prized, begging a similar one to send home. She courteously affected gratitude for all, but the French buttons were soon lost, and the German cap was thrown upon a dust heap. Her interest was in the kind of dinners they got in the intervals of war. Men had to eat whether English or Germans, and she supposed there was a set dinner hour for all. Willie explained. To think that there was no such hour shocked her almost to incredulity, but she endorsed the quoted maxim of an old soldier – 'Meat for them as wants it: juice for me!' Let the youngsters crowd round the 'dixy' for lumps! He would dip his bread in what was left – the liquid.

'And he knowed,' said Dorothy with approval. 'Always you do the same, Master Willie!'

He left her brooding over the possibility of turning old hens into delicious chicken by burying them (feathers and all) in the ground for a fortnight before cooking – which thing was done in Flanders, when fortune favoured the troops.

Then he wallowed in the luxury of a hot bath, and reappeared forty minutes later in a dressing gown to eat beef steak, and drink cider unchilled by immersion of a crust toasted before the greatly rejoicing fire of old pear wood.

He and his mother talked till midnight – an unheard of hour! Then, cool sheets! candle-light flickering upon familiar books and pictures: the sweet noise of wind in orchards: sleep unbroken through fifteen hours.

About three o'clock on the following afternoon he got up, angry with himself for so remaining unconscious of his joy during those many hours of sleep, but mightily refreshed.

He sat with his mother, or followed her about the house all that day, and they talked out their hearts to good purpose, lightening each soul and enriching it, by a double exchange.

Concealing none of war's horrors (since to veil is to magnify) he spoke frankly of happiness found in army discipline. 'You see,' he said, 'it is the symbol, which has caused me to understand you and Eric and all who have thrown care upon God and made Him 'responsible' as it were, in return for service. One does not argue beyond choosing one's cause on enlisting. After that it is just obeying orders. The end is not with you. So one is not proud with success, nor despondent for lack of it. Success is not your affair – only to do what you are command. And this breeds a careless energy impossible in others, and a happiness due to never unduly pondering the riddles of strategy which need be solved through but not by you. Our chaplain hit it off once in a daring phrase.'

'Remember', he said, 'that if you are responsible, God is infinitely more so! And He loves you.'

'Whether our war-lords also love us is a debatable point, but the first half of that saying remains true. Our responsibility is obedience. That, of course, would be an intolerable thing, were it it not for the first voluntary choice of 'the cause.'

'As for me, I have never worked my body so hard: risked it so wantonly: or fretted it with so many annoyances. But my soul has not been disquieted: my thoughts have not been over-clouded with anxieties. I have not fretted my mind. And oh, what relief it is from the misery and doubt and fret of my former existence, Mother!'

'My darling!'

'There is energy in peace. It is creative. There is no creative energy but in peace. When a man has solved his problems or (as we have done) brushed them aside, he can put himself into his work – himself and something else. But a distracted men puts only half of himself into his labour, and that half is poisoned. It is closed also to that more important thing than mere self which comes to help happy men. A tortured man can't open his heart. He fears something will stab it. Yet grace comes only to those who do so. And grace is that which lifts man to anything greater than he is. You can call it grace or you can call it inspiration. It is the outer help and it applies equally to religion and literature.'

'That is true, dear.'

'Eric and I have approached peace from different sides. Yet we have come to the same kind of creed – "Whoso loseth his life shall find it." It may not be the same kind of life that he and I shall lose. It cannot be, either one way or the other – but the end is happiness, and creation. Of that (whether we live or die) I am sure: for in a sense, we are both dead, and have found peace already. Our bodies – our rum wonderful old bodies – remain. But if they die, and peace will only be the greater – and the creative possibilities also.'

Then, smiling, 'this talk of mine is becoming sermony. I must visit Eric some time and sacrifice to his rum old body a drink of rum. I can't go back "there" without seeing him,' he added.

'No, dear. And he would love to see you. You could go Friday. That's your last day but one, isn't it?' (as if she, who was counting the days in her heart, didn't know this!)

'Yes.'

'Then you can come back home, and put on clean underclothes to go out in.'

Willie smiled. 'All right, darling.'

'And how is the regimental paper going on?' asked his mother. 'I meet many old friends in it – poems of yours written long ago.'

'Yes, I have had to use them up when topical matters ran short. They are often more suitable, since they deal with things which soldiers think of more often than they think of war – the county; the things they loved in peace; all that they are fighting for.'

'Those are the ones I like best' answered his mother.

'Yes, with stray exceptions such as 'Gonnehem', 'If we return', and 'In Flanders', they are the best, and the strange thing is that since this regimental gazette of ours has become famous – for apparently it has – those same poems are seized upon and published with high approval by the same English papers and magazines which formerly refused them. To be passionately fond of England is a literary virtue in war-time, but so provincial in peace! Yet who would write of England at all except for that peaceful England – this England of quiet lives, and misty orchards? What man in his senses would risk life for that other fretful, profiteering, foolish, feverish place? No, Mother, I don't value at twopence this new craze, but I am going to take advantage of it: even if I am called a soldier-poet, as if there were such a thing, or ever could be anything else than men whose call is to poetry in peace or war, and men whose call is to other things – poets or not poets ...

'I have been lucky. I have got a decoration –'

'Will that help you, dear?'

'Enormously. It will seem so strange to these people to find any-body without knock-knees and long hair writing verse. That is what they imagine a poet is. They don't care for poetry, any more than they care for bravery. What they want is sensation ...

These are my children. I have no more than these – my poems. I am going to give them a good start in life. I am going to drive in a blow for my England, while the Philistines' guard is down, and the aesthete hidden in the conservatory, alone (for once) with his languid lilies. I shall hit 'em both hard on the jaw, and go back to France feel-ing that I don't care much whether I live or die.'

'But how?' asked Mrs. Harvey.

'That', said Willie, 'is a little surprise. I wanted to tell you myself, and didn't mention in my letters that a book of your old friends – your little grandchildren, is to be published by a very well-known London firm this month!'

'My dear, I am so glad!'

'Yes, it's good, isn't it? And what a joke!'

'I don't think it a joke, dearest. I think you have come into your own. If this horrible war has allowed it (as you say) then I have one single cause for blessing it.'

'Thank you for them kind words ma'am,' he laughed.

CHAPTER IV

Willie, with a great hamper of his mother's, and a little ivory rosary which was his own gift to Eric, rode to the railway station on Friday morning in a carrier's van.

A buzz of local gossip sounded beneath that weather-stained hood above the rumble of wheels. It was the sort of talk which may still be heard in any country place throughout Severn Vale, and it echoed and re-echoed like music in Willie's ears, and in memory long after that misty autumn day had gone.

Greeting from those who knew him (e.e. almost everyone) were quickly followed by all sorts of enquiries concerning his recent experiences, and many quaint condemnations of 'they malice-minded baggers' – the enemy. Willie turned the talk into natural channels with questions of his own concerning crops and relatives.

'Aye, a goodish summer, but now' ('twas held) 'weather would turn dabbledey.'

'A good fruit harvest anyway.'

'Aye, a great 'bundation o' fruit, but few to pick it; the lads being gone to war. And there was nobody to put rungs in the daddocky ladders since carpenters were shorthanded too. Gaffer Herrige did vaal drow only 'tothey day and break his leg at ninety. But worser nor that did happen at the war they reckoned and many was the poor lad as 'ud be glad to be whoam a-picking. (Chorus of aye! aye!) It did seem sort of unreasonable o' Providence to send war and quantities of apples together. Many did mind years when there had been no apples at all to pick. Then there was plenty of "buoys", all eating their yuds off.'

'How is old Gaffer Herrige going on?' asked Willie.

Mending rare – a wonder among ancient men.'

'Zo', jealously cried Bill Hatchet, 'zo be my old uncle Zamuel a wonder. 'Twould surprise ye neighbours to hear how careful we got to be wi' 'ee. Ninety dree a be, and can't zee much. But can't a hear! You got to be careful when he's about I tell 'ee. He'll hear anything.

And smell! Golly can't a smell! He do smell everything as soon as ever it do come into the house. Like a dog.'

'A wer a gurt cheeze-smeller in his time, an did judge 'em at shows, I do mind' commented a friend.

'Zo a did, and maybe that accounts. Still, a be a wonderful mon' repeated Hatchet.

All this Willie noted, and thought how amused Eric would be at the retailing of it that afternoon in camp. The roadside elms loomed shadowy standing in circles of condensed moisture. Two leisurely trotting horses sent smoky breath before them. Mist wrapped the meadows, lying in long banks as they approached winding Severn. Mist lay like white music upon Piper's Wood.

'Your little Polly has grown into a big girl Mrs. Handscombe.'

'Aye, Maaster Willie, she have growed. She be a rare gurt flitchen I can tell 'ee. And she do sing like a bird.'

'That's nice.'

'She allus wer one to sing. I mind when I took her to church fust time, the christening except. Her couldn't read at all, but a took a book and sang so as to astonish everybody. "What be you a singing now?" I axed her. "You don't know no words" I said. 'I do make they up, Mother' said she.'

'Ha, ha, ha' laughed the company.

'Well, take care of the sounds and the sense will take care of itself' quoted Willie, but the jest passed unheeded.

'Thy Feyther could allus carry a song, I mind' put in another woman. 'Tis a gift I reckon.'

'Aye, that a could. Many's the harvest whoam I've heard un raise wi' a's voice:–

'Ploughed well, sowed well;
Reaped well, mowed well'
Carried well, housed well;
Nur' a load overdrowd:
Harvest Whoam!'

'A had another song a called 'Riddle cum Ruddle', but I do verget the words on't' put in a voice. 'It did make 'un very dry.'

'Aye, a singing mon do need liquor.'

'That be natur' agreed the rest.

'So do ringing too!' cried excitedly one of bulk bearing upon tremendous shoulders the kindly face of an October sunset: 'So do ringers need liquor. And I knows it: for after the new parson come and forbade our lil' cask in the tower, none on us had hardly spit in his mouth to wet his hands for a grip on the rope.'

('Aye sure! Aye sure!' was chorused around.)

'Though 'twer hardly right on 'Arry to call un to a's face a whey-faced old sod' he added. (This motion also was carried unanimously.)

A distant threshing machine hummed like a gigantic bee. This sound faded. Trotting hoofs and such talk as before persisted upon the ear. Occasionally the hoot-toot of a motor, or faster-beating hoofs came up in a crescendo, and diminished. Silence fell upon the occupants of the van.

'How is Will Jacks?' asked Willie, thinking silence sweet, but speech better, in such company.

The Cathedral hove in sight round that turning of the road past Over bridge. Severn was crossed. Soon in Westgate Street of Gloucester city, all would disperse to sell and 'shop'.

'Will Jacks – no good on as ever. His feyther did hang hisself, and there be some as do wish as 'e ud do the same. A' do cruelly intreat his wife who do go about (poor creytur) looking like the jaws o' Death.'

This terrific phrase was the last to be culled by Willie on his way to town. Folks began gathering their parcels and baskets together. The van pulled up at 'The White Swan'. Its occupants disappeared, calling encouraging remarks. Willie shouldering his hamper made hurriedly for the station.

Catching his train, he reached Ludgershall after a tiresome journey and set out to find the camp and his brother. Small beauty that soaking day was on Salisbury Plain to set beside Minsterworth and the misty orchards! A bleak unbroken landscape met his gaze. He trudged on through mud, slush and water, to a spot where long ugly huts and tents tearing out their pegs by contraction of the grey ropes denoted the presence of a regiment. His shoulder ached with the weight of the hamper, but he marched joyously and with little scorn of surroundings. He was going to see Eric. Soon they would be talking together in some canteen. It was not from fatigue alone that he found himself trembling as he dropped his load within the lines of his reserve battalion. After enquiring at one or two tents he made for the orderly room. Harvey: Private Harvey, number 3285.

A list was consulted. Yes, Private Harvey had gone on a draft to France the night before.

Willie, leaving the hamper to be shared among his brother's old tent companions, and with the little rosary like lead in his pocket, set off upon his homeward journey. A day wasted ...

He arrived back in the early hours of the following day, feeling as weary as he had felt upon his return from the front – and a lot less joyous.

Standing outside his home that was humped like a sleeping animal against the eerie beginnings of early dawn, Willie with memory of his disappointment and foreboding of his own departure in his heart felt that beauty had withdrawn even from this spot so dear, so lovely. An atmosphere of death seemed to dwell upon it.

He threw gravel at the window of his mother's room. He heard her answer, and saw colour kindling as she lighted a candle to come down. The whole thing seemed to have happened before (as he knew that after death it would again) and he waited to carry out that symbolic ritual which he knew was unfolding. Bearing a light which shone upon her face his mother, having descended the stairs from her bedroom, passed the hall window and peered through to see that it was really her son who stood waiting to enter. Her face paused against the glass. He bent forward (as he knew he must) to kiss it, and feeling only the cold barrier, burst into tears. This was foolish. He felt that all the time. but something was driving him and all the time he knew too that what had happened before, and would happen again, must happen now. His mother would open the door, and finding him in tears would kiss him and take him in. Then all the horrible eerie loneliness would vanish. He would have come home. He would be happy – happy.

'Well dearest, back again, and very tired!'

The strange vision fled with that spoken welcome. Dream no longer perched upon reality. Brushing his eyes, he entered the familiar house, and told his tale, she sitting in her dressing gown to listen, as he sipped his hot drink and ate bread and butter.

'Well, well, it had to be sooner or later' said his mother. 'He was wanting so much to get out to you. And now you will see him there instead of in England – long before I can' she added wistfully.

'Yes, Mother, and though I loathe leaving you I am almost glad to be going back to-morrow.'

'To-day', corrected she, 'it is morning. And now you must go to bed, poor boy, and get a bit of rest before your travel!'

'I suppose I must, Mother.'

He arose, and they went upstairs – he to sleep soundly, and she to lie awake praying, as thousands of other mothers prayed to God that night ... in many countries.

The same morning at eleven o'clock he shouldered his pack, slung his rifle, and left his home behind. That night at Victoria Station he met hundreds of other returning soldiers. It was a strange sight – that huge roofed-in place of departure – at this time. None who have travelled in a 'leave train' will ever forget it. Smoke and arches blotting out the stars; a cavern of crowded and very various loves – a terminus of so much life, yet nothing like life: a starting point for death, yet nothing like death. A ball-room of half-naked emotions in fantastic dances!

What a company had assembled! Of women - pale, weeping girls, and laughing prostitutes, and courageously smiling mothers. Of men – fathers trying to be matter of fact, friends, and brothers affecting cheeriness, and soldiers of all sorts and conditions and in every mood of parting – cheerily or gloomily sober: gloomily or cheerily intoxicated. A.S.C. men boasting of the blood they would shed in France: Pay Office clerks who promised German helmets on their return: privates of the infantry repeating mechanically trivial messages which would be treasured – or not – when they were dead.

Snaps of comedy and of tragedy floated here and there upon general flood of talk. In that feverish expectancy of parting restraints became unendurable and were dissipated. Even self-controlled men spoke with trembling tones and tears in their eyes their last goodbyes to those from whose hearts the veil of reticence slipped with the moments.

The low whispering grew louder and at length desperately careless. Who listened? What mattered even if they did?

The half-lighted train, which had lain so quiet, now snorted like a gigantic sinister beast, and prepared to depart.

'All aboard for Berlin!' 'Goodbye, mother!' Cheerio old thing!' 'A V.C. next time.' 'Stop her, she's got my purse: every bloody sou!' 'Darling, I don't care. It will be yours, yours whether we've been to the church or not.' 'Look after Dicky!' 'Where's my blasted haversack?' 'Another kiss then!' Goodbye! Goodbye! Goodbye!' Sobs, cheering, broken shouts The train moves slowly out. 'Thank God that's over!' 'Good old Blighty!' 'Where's my ...' Men settle in their seats and look at one another ...

'She is alone' thought Willie of his mother. 'We are both alone, but I am on my way to meet Eric. That's not so bad is it? And I said goodbye to her in Gloucestershire – quietly.'

'Have a swig, mate?'

'Not now, old man, thanks.'

'Come on; be matey!' hiccoughed one drowning care.

'Keep it for the crossing, and the cold night' advised Willie, sipping, and handing back the flask.

'No fear!' answered the soldier, draining the whole contents of spirit prior to falling asleep.

Food was taken from haversacks and handed round, but nobody wanted to eat. It was a token of friendliness; no more; and the ritual accomplished, all snatched a chance to sleep with exception of four gamblers bunched together in the middle of the carriage, and Willie in one corner.

The train rocked on through the darkness. Willie watched the faces around him – and sleeping and the waking. Were these the saviours of England? How queer to think so! But it was true. Life (he mused) must mean something very different to each one of these men. The thing in common: and the thing which set them in dignity apart from so much wiser and more clever men, was the hazard of it. It was not mere shillings and francs that these boys were gambling with. They, he and those sleepers, had chosen, one and all, a larger game ... gamblers all, they were! Time alone would show if the game were worth the playing. But time could never rob the players of their nobleness. The shame (if shame should be the end of this adventure) would never touch them. It would lie upon others – the onlookers – the wise, the clever men in England and elsewhere then abed, dreaming their wise, clever dreams.

He rubbed the moisture of breath from the window pane, and looked out, but there was nothing to be seen – not even the passing telegraph poles. He thought of his leave and saw with the mind's eye the faces he had left behind. He heard the Gloucestershire talk ... Then he took from his pocket a sealed envelope given him by Dorothy in the moment of departure. Now what's this? A love letter? He broke the seal and read. Dear folks! Dear, dear Gloucestershire folks! Tears came into his eyes as he laughed and laughed.

'What's up chum? Got hold of a smart tale? Got a good joke to tell us?' questioned the gambling enthusiasts. The sleepers wriggled and snorted at the noise and turned back into dreams.

'No,' said Willie, 'not a story, but a joke if you see it right.'

'When you fellows are back in trenches, and suffering any manner of cold: perhaps lying out on listening patrol and wanting to cough, only afraid to, and feeling your throat tickling like mad all the time – here's a remedy.'

'Place four new-laid eggs in a basin' ('Wot the 'ell?' began one of his listeners.) 'Cover with the juice of six lemons' (Mr Mill's might do) 'and leave for twenty-four hours.' (You'll be a bit stiff and cold by that when) 'turn the eggs over and leave for another twenty-four hours'. ('Oh Gawd!' exclaimed one. 'Shall we never be allowed in agen!') 'then beat up with four ounces of honey, and one and a half ounces of glycerine and three-quarters of a bottle of rum' (Wot will the sergeant say!) 'Strain through a muslin, and then bottle. Does one wineglass' concluded Willie.

'Now that's an infallible cure for colds, revealed only to us five by Dorothy's old mother who has dosed her husband with same for years, and got it from her mother.'

'Where did she get the eggs from?'

'I've noticed streams o' blinkin' honey running about Plug Street Wood.'

'You'd 'ave to save your rum during the first ten years o' war – them as they says will be the worst too – if you didn't 'appen to be a sergeant.'

'Well, that's the only cure anyhow' said Willie.

Warmed even with the thought of that recipe Willie crossed the channel (two long destroyers like grey shadows accompanying) and landed again on French soil.

CHAPTER V

'Behold two happy mortals upon a road that leads God knows where.'

Three days before, Eric had come over on the same ship, and had proceeded up the line with thirty odd companions, occupying a cattle trench labelled thus – '8 chevaux, 40 hommes'

'Pity we ain't chevauxes, mate. Eight on us could stretch out nice on this straw', said a soldier to Etic.

'There isn't much room for nearly forty chaps' agreed Eric.

'There', cried another, 'I said hommes was a misprint for tommies. That's what they call us out 'ere.'

'It's like living in a gypsy van', remarked somebody.

'Indeed it isn't!' cried out a slim dark-haired boy squeezed into a further corner. There was something in the tone that made Eric ask 'Have you ever lived in one?' And there was a slight hesitation ere out of the shadow the voice replied 'No – only I've known people who have.'

'Gypsies?'

'There's plenty of people travel that way, besides gypsies.'

Eric thought it tactful not to pursue the subject. The boy was enough like a gypsy himself. He had appeared from nowhere to enlist about five months previously in the reserve battalion of Gloucesters. His accent was only faintly of the west, and while he knew many places of the country he would never admit that his home was in any of them, and no one could recognise him as a native. He learned quickly, was a good scout, and had voluntarily taken the place of another man who was booked for this draft but whose mother had fallen ill, thereby gaining the regard of his present companions who had, with the majority, mistrusted him hitherto, and called him 'foreigner'.

His taciturnity had somewhat thawed during this journey, and he had betrayed signs of excitement which might have puzzled his companions, had they not been somewhat excited themselves. Not one of these men grudged himself to this adventure, yet each felt a deep sadness at leaving 'for foreign parts', and his excitement was feeding both on the thought that he was now on his way to the line, and on the apprehension that he would never return from it. This excitement was covered with jests, amusing criticism of the French country and its people, and the intermittent grousing which is Tommie's privilege. But such was not the excitement of 'the foreigner'.

The train pulled up in a wood, and an order was given that the soldiers might 'fall out', stretch their legs, and eat dinner in its covering shade.

Eric took advantage of the stop to write a letter home:–

'My dearest: You will be surprised to hear that I am on my way to the front, and at the moment (I believe) only a dozen miles off it; so that I shall soon see Willie and give him your love. It was a rather sudden departure or I would have let you know before – but our letters would have been held up anyway I think. You have heard all about the country from Willie, so I will say no more than that I am well and happy. I shall continue to be the latter whether I live or die, for it is in me, and never more than at the present. Do not grieve if I tell you that it is also in my bones that I shall not see you again – alive. I had planned much that I hoped to carry out, but nothing better than this – to yield myself soul and body to the will of God in crusade. His will only be done. In that be our joy! So may His kingdom come on earth as it is in Heaven.

Ever your loving Son,

ERIC.'

He was lying on the straw of the truck reading a pocket Bible and smiling happing to himself when the other returned after the 'Fall-in' whistle had sounded.

'Well, you look happy enough!' remarked his neighbour as he settled beside him. 'Yes' said Eric.

'Well, I reckon we may just as well take what comes smiling,' rejoined the other, 'but ty-unt going to be a picnic either.'

'I know that.'

'You be religious' said the man, glancing at Eric's book. 'No offence. I don't mean parsonish. 'Tis reasonable for a man as do understand about Heaven to be happy whether a be gwaine to die or live –'

'It is!' said Eric.

'But the foreigner there', whispered the soldier and jerking his head towards the opposite corner – 'he bain't religious, and ... and I seen him do queer things in that 'ood.'

'What queer things?'

'Like this – I had yut my bit o' bait, and wer lying quiet under a bush, thinking how the 'ood were like a little 'un I knowed at home; when the foreigner comes out upon a little bare place where the sun did lie in a patch with trees all round. My bush was under oe 'em. And just as I wer going to call out to 'un, well ...'

'Well?'

'A started dancing.'

'How dancing?'

'Dancing (though t'wasn't no ordinary dance like) in the sunshine and singing a scrap o' music as though a was glad!'

'Perhaps he was glad.'

'Maybe. And a held out a's arms as though a wer welcoming summat, or somebody that a could see – though there wer nothing there. Then a broke dro' the bushes, and wer gone afore I could say a word good or bad.'

'Ah!'

'It's come to me while we bin a talking, as that there foreigner were a music hall chap, a play actor, or dancer like as had got no home to remember and long for, like; and must go back in his mind to what a did know best – the dancing a did.'

'You think it was done because of a sort of home-sickness?'

'That dome to me since I bin talking. Afore that, I thought a must be mad. He seemed zo glad-like.'

'Perhaps,' repeated Eric, 'he was glad.'

'Why?'

'To be going to meet what fate brings to him.'

'That we must face.'

'Gladly.'

'Well, I dunno, A man may be glad meeting friends, or meeting his sweetheart, or coming home, but we beyunt doing neither!'

'We are meeting what God sends.'

'Ah, you be religious. Yet you don't dance. He bain't religious. But he do. He's a music-haller.'

'Well, perhaps you're right.'

'And you see!'

The shadows of the truck grew darker. Evening and a few stars had come when the train presently stopped, having reached its farthest limit of safety.

As the men fell in their places to march off Eric's companion placed himself next to the foreigner. 'You wasn't on the halls, mate, before you come 'ere?' he asked.

'The what?'

'The halls. A hactor, or anything?'

'No!' laughed the other. And they marched on in silence till they reached a spot closely in rear of the lines. But there they were not destined to remain.

'Now you're for it, chums!' came the voice of their guide. They marched on in darkness into reserve trenches, where duck boards broke, periodically letting them down into icy water. One man broke his leg, and so left the war before he had seen it. Then they reached a spot where for a winding mile Frenchmen were stuck, and moved neither forward nor backward.

That was an atmosphere of oaths, if you like!

'What's up?'

Answers were many, but unprintable.

'Better get out of this and go across country', said the guide; but as he spoke the air filled with a whistling which became a scream. Synchronised to a second the German guns opened fire.

Like a monstrous covey of birds those wings beating the darkness came to earth. The shrieking, the whistling, the scream with which the air throbbed agonised, was overborne in a blast of hell. The shout of ten million demons rent the sky. Earth swayed; gathered into waves; spouted fountains of itself – and other things more precious than dirt.

The scream of those birds of death was echoed back from throats of living and dying men … Then as a mine was fired, the buried were shaken in their tombs like dice; and amongst them was 'the foreigner'.

Not a shot was fired back. What had those poor miserable men to fire at? The scream of our own shells crossed them crowded there, or sprawling in blood, or lying grotesquely dismembered. Defiance, courage, devilry, bravery, counted for nothing. It was flesh and blood and valiant spirit against iron: bloody machinery. It was modern war.

The artillery duel continued as an attack was made upon the English trenches. Our barrage wiped out the attacks. The defenders were wiped out by German shells which murdered and buried them. The reserves on both sides suffered a similar fate, but in a lesser measure. This trench of men was perhaps decimated.

Shovels, not rifles, were wanted; and fortunately these were to hand. They dug out their own men, and then in darkness dug out covering for themselves, and a new front line, the result being that neither army had advanced a single inch by daylight, and each had caught but casual and fleeting glimpses of the other. No one could be firmly conscious of having killed a single man. Yet casualties on both sides were heavy – about even.

Of many acts of unrecorded heroism in truth performed under secrecy of covering darkness it is duty to relate but one.

In that purgatory of flame, burning flesh, smoke, spouting dirt: in those rising cries of agony; in that rain of descending death-giving shells: Eric stood up and found a shovel. Then, without waiting for a lull, he dug. He dug out a human form buried in French earth that else would have remained there till the day of Doom. It was (though he knew not) 'the foreigner'. And meanwhile, for it was death to do it, men marvelled, and he was untouched. A hand guarded him.

('If anybody deserved a V.C. that madman does.')

He aided them in remaking their trench, and the levelled trench in front. 'My brother is there alive, or dead,' was the thought that ran in his mind. But furious digging did not reveal his brother, and he fell asleep exhausted on the soft wet earth which lay around his spade.

In the morning people recognised him. His brother was on leave – lucky bounder! His brother's pals were mostly dead, or wounded. He was welcomed by the rest, and put on the roll.

'You'll meet him to-morrow night' said the sergeant, 'and then we're going to give 'Jerry' what for over this, and he'll help us to: don't you forget it. Who's your friend in the shining buttons?' pointing to the foreigner.

'That's Private Gain. He was buried last night and hasn't been so clean since.'

'He dug me out, Sergeant.'

'Good lad! So now you're a Private Gain 'stead of a public loss, eh?' replied that great man, and departed to take the names of the other newcomers. But of thirty-five that had sailed from England a couple of days before only fifteen had arrived in the front line.

CHAPTER VI

Viewed with the eye of imagination, or even photographed from an aeroplane, the countryside appeared very differently than to the eye of an infantryman in trenches.

That eye when was not glued to a periscope was exploring some twenty to fifty yards of heaped-up dirt and sand-bags – The radius of his particular section to whom the trench was a village street: home: a temporary shelter from death. He might know a little of the villages beyond, held by the next section, or platoon. Curiosity as to the general lie of the land, or even the bends of the hostile trench was repaid instantly with death: a bullet through the head.

The periscope showed a tangle of enemy wire. The naked eye saw besides walls of riveted earth, nothing save flowers of sleep – the plentiful red poppies which crept even to the brink of this hiding place – a double symbol, of bloodshed by their hue; of sleep by extract and significance. Beside this, the strip of blue or sodden sky that bent above, earth underfoot; these and faces that would ere long gaze upon all mysteries and symbols of life and death with greater understanding: faces which would be trampled, polluted into dark dirt, lit with spirit which would shine serenely with the stars in purple skies, or grieve in rain beholding the betrayal of their dreams: which would eat of the soul of the poppy, and rest, yet not unconsciously of such things as they had loved.

Poppies, a strip of sky, and dirt in a protecting wall, was for their eyes: a sickening stench of unburied flesh for their smell: flesh that no longer bore semblance of humanity: rat-gnawed, green, distended with corruption: bladders of foulness from which the hair rotted in rain and wind: bones and stink in particles dug up and put into sand-bags for a weak wall against the bullet that had pierced them.

Sleep-flowers, a ribbon of sky; and sodden earth for their eyes, stink for their nostrils; terror for their hearing – the scream and bursting of shell, the whizz and whine of the bullet. This in a narrow area of fifty yards, was that each man knew. This was his home – the home of the infantry in two armies.

But from the air, a mere photograph gives unity to a larger scene, showing miles of trenches like scratches upon a pock-marked surface, bending, following one another in lines more or less parallel – A the German front line: B the British.

Behind these, hundreds of intersecting scratches like forked lightning where action has been caught, and stamped upon the plate of a camera – the communication trenches, and those of supporting troops. And between them always the same bald, scarred and pitted face of death, dignified by the name of French: her wide war zone blasted, shorn, pimpled and disfigured with every scab and boil of murder.

To such a place had come Eric and his companions when poppies were dead, the skies hard with the first cold. In such sheltering they were rejoined by Willie on his return to the front some twenty-four hours after.

The trench had been consolidated (a good word!) and preparations were in full swing for the return attack, raid, or whatever it might turn out to be – that is, for a new slaughtering of men.

Willie was slopping up the trench looking for his brother when our guns started in a hubbub of explosions like the rather bad start of drunken giants in a sprint. The race went by in a scream to the tape – or rather the enemy entanglements. One or two missed their footing as they ran and fell with a crash dangerously near our own trenches. Scraps of iron torn like tissue paper came whizzing back, causing new arrived heads to duck (as if that were any use!) Then immediately more races were run by the giants. So the Germans started theirs, retaliating not upon the guilty artillery responsible for all this, but upon our reserve and front-line trenches.

This continued for half an hour. Meanwhile Willie had found Eric. Speech was impossible in that hellish din. They gripped hands, and waited side by side upon the fire-step for 'zero' when the assault would be made. And with them, waited 'the foreigner', whom Eric had dug out the day before.

'We'd be a sight safer in 'no-man's-land' than here' yelled Willie to the Sergeant who was passing. He guessed rather than heard the words, and passed on the saying to the officer. He agreed, but his instructions were to remain where enemy shells were falling rather than where they would pass over head. He could give no orders other than those we had received. Yet the mere instinct of self-preservation caused that manoeuvre to be carried out. As their trench crumbled and fell in men crept gradually in ones and twos into shell holes, and when zero was signalled three parts of what remained of two assaulting battalions were already half way across No-man's-land, and within twenty yards of the enemy wire.

They were first through it and into the enemy trench which was of course empty save for a few machine gunners who surrendered or were bayonetted. Then in a wave the British passed on to the trenches beyond, but found them strongly held, and their protecting were almost intact.

The assault upon these continued through the night and was a complete failure. The order for retirement when given was heard only by about half of those who remained alive, and dawn saw the remainder firing in small scattered bodies from holes, or hung up on wire entanglements. They were enfiladed from two sides and all but surrounded since the Germans had pushed troops along the old front-line trench, a great part of which was already repaired, and occupied.

The enemy had, in fact, succeeded in bombing our troops from all but a short stretch in the centre; which was now doomed to be squeezed out by pressure on its flanks.

But the scattered fighters between the first and second German lines, had no knowledge of this. They supposed that their own reserves were occupying the old German line, over which they had passed the night before.

Light showed clearly enough that their present attack upon the German reserve lines was over, and had failed. Light showed the mud-smeared faces of Willie, Eric, and the foreigner gazing at one another in a great shell-hole, which was half full of icy water. They lapped it occasionally, for though their limbs were sodden enough their throats were parched, and water bottles had not been filled for twenty-four hours. Light spread, gilding the surface of pools which had long since drowned the wounded. It revealed thick bushes of enemy wire heavy with their fruit of death – men caught and hanging, shot through and through: men without arms: men without heads: and one who faintly moved in spasms, and squeaked – no more than that!

It was Willie who first spoke. 'We must get back at once. What a mess! What a hopeless, dreadful ...' He stopped, seeing the face of

Private Gain raised to the light. 'I've seen you before' he said. 'Now where was it?'

'In the Forest of Dean' came the whispered answer. 'And again in Cotswold.'

'Good God!' cried Willie. 'It is my gypsy girl!'

Eric gave an exclamation of surprise, and stared fixedly upon the pale dishevelled foreigner before him. Then, 'And I never guessed it!' muttered he. 'But how? … Why?' …

'We must go!' she said, and crawled over the edge of the shell-hole. Willie wriggled after her. Eric lifted his head and then sprawled back into the hole having taken the bullet meant for his brother. In a flash both were beside him, lifting his poor head and speaking to him in vain. 'He is dead' said the girl. 'It is (weeping) as it was to be.'

'I'll have blood for this!' shouted he. And at that moment spiked helmets appeared above the rim of sheltering earth and a voice bade them in guttural tones to surrender.

Will raised his rifle. His companion sprang upon it. He wrenched it savagely away to aim, but her weight was upon it, directing the muzzle downward. He dropped the weapon and struck her with his fist full on the forehead. Germans tumbled in upon what was apparently a madman and two dead companions. The madman was quickly reduced to quiet insensibility with the butt of a rifle.

PART VI

CAPTURED

CHAPTER I

That the butt of a German rifle is harder than any naked fist, was a thought which occurred to Willie when he woke again in a dug out of wounded prisoners upon whom 'Private Gain' had been detailed to wait as an orderly.

The gypsy girl went to and fro with water and bandages. Her forehead carried a bruise as big as a hen's egg. Willie's had been laid by a much larger bird – a swan at least!

He opened his lids and watched her walking towards him dressed in a muddy British uniform of a private soldier. Thoughts crowded his brain. Visions arose before him of Jean Foust, a gypsy fire, a girl of arresting beauty, a visit with Eric and that swarthy man – her father – to the cave of Christ a-weeping. He saw steep windy Cotswold; on it himself a wanderer; then suddenly a sacred vision of beauty in the moonlight; a wide-blown dress moulding the shape of a mortal girl who talked to him in splintered shade and light of woodlands. He beheld the dawn-gilded horrors of No-man's-land where recognition had taken place – he, and she, and Eric, in a shell-hole half full of icy water; death around: the final scene: Eric dead beside him: Madness! ...

His lids closed. He drank water from a bottle she held to his lips; hearing the few words she spoke, but understanding nothing. How? and Why? were circles of fire that blazed in his head. Wheels of flame, they turned, and left him in darkness.

A German feldwebel came round, raking down in a little book the names, numbers, and regiments, which were printed upon their identification disks.

After that a German officer of the medical corps examined them hastily, and pronounced Willie and some others including 'the foreigner' fit to walk. They were helped up with rifle butts, and given in charge of two armed soldiers, one of whom marched before, and one behind the party, as it filed down the deep and muddy communication trench.

Willie's next neighbour in the march was a private in the Berkshires who had been captured in the same manner as himself – islanded as it were, in seas of hostile and friendly bullets.

'It wasn't fighting one way. The sods was all round. Only a human corkscrew could manage 'em – and his flesh turned steel armour. Our own chaps was firing on us as hard as they:– blast their silly eyes!'

'They didn't know they were hitting us,' apologised Willie.

'No,' said his neighbour thoughtfully, 'and how the hell we got there I don't know.'

It was a summary of that day's military situation.

'What funny uniforms these German do wear!' he remarked later, jerking a thumb at the grey-clad figure behind.

Reaching the main road, they were herded into the court-yard of a great French mansion. 'Achtung!' They were kicked to attention. A German officer, or more accurately OFFICER, inspected them. His rank may have been anything from lieutenant to general. He was fat. His chin bulged in a pink slab over his collar. His age was about forty.

Willie felt a momentary touch on his arm, and heard a quick whisper in his ear – 'Farm labourer!' – as 'the foreigner' passed to take her place in the line.

The OFFICER (followed by an officer) then checked the names, numbers, and regiments of the prisoners, and enquired of each his civilian occupation.

'Farm-labourer' answered Willie obediently.

The farm-labourers were divided off from the rest and marched away.

That night was spent in a guarded loft above stables of a farm house which was occupied by German artillery.

Six British soldiers listened to the crunch-munching of horses which was the night's most continuous sound only broken by irregular explosions of falling shells, and the reply of adjacent cannon. Horses are the same all over the world over.

To Willie (and doubtless to the rest) it was music which breathed of home – this sleepy munch of mouths, and occasional movement of hoofs beneath. But thoughts kept him awake. Thoughts, and possibly hunger, kept awake also his companions, long after their first German meal of malodorous vegetable soup, and brown sticky bread had been swallowed, and the basins handed back to the sentry standing outside.

It was four o'clock and a finger of faint wire-barred moonlight with-drawing from the loft, when someone moving stealthily among uneasy sleepers came to his side. He guessed who. But, heavy with memories of Eric's unavenged death, he made no answer to her whispers. It was no fit of sulkiness. He felt simply that he could not speak to her. Yet he felt shame at having struck her, and a devouring curiosity as to her presence. – 'Go away!' he said. And she obeyed, as he had previously obeyed her, in answering the Germans as to his occupation.

But next morning she stood next to him in the line that was formed outside in the yard. She also it was who asked the German OFFICER that the prisoners should be permitted to write home. The request was refused. But Willie was grateful to her, guessing that she would have no need of such permission but was reminding him of a duty to his mother which grief had made him forget.

It was early morning. The mist-wet roofs of house, barn, and sta-bles, had turned to some precious metal under sunrise. the buildings stood in a square enfolding the yard, French fashion. In the middle of the square upon the heaped-up midden, a cock stood up, crowed, and flapped glittering wings like a herald of something or somebody mysterious and unknown. A dog tread-milled round and round a great wheel whose axle worked – a churn perhaps – inside the adjoin-ing wall of the house. A small Madonna and Child set high in a little glass-covered niche on the same building was caught and coloured by early sunbeams.

German soldiers, washing without enthusiasm around the pump, turned mockingly to grin at the khaki-clad man – or shouted insults.

Orders were given by a feldwebel who strutted up and down the line: each man was supplied with a slice of bread: the party was marched off under charge of armed guards to a railway station. Then, as marked off by the feldwebel the prisoners were separated into couples, Willie and his accomplice being made mates.

They were bound for German farms whose owners had applied for labour: such help being granted by the Government in cases where additional aid was necessary owing to sons or employers having been called to the war.

For many hours the party travelled together. First to break off was our friend of the Berkshires and his mate. Willie and his compan-ion were given in charge of a landsturm soldier at the next station. The following night, after another train journey, they arrived, almost famished, at the gefangenenlager which supplied British labour to that district of German farms.

The prison was a rectangular wind-in space containing four long huts made of match-boarding covered with tarred felt. Sentries and electric lamps were stationed at intervals outside the wire. The new arrivals were detailed to hut number four, where they received a kindly and hospitable welcome from seven older prisoners – four English soldiers, two Scottish, and one Irish; all except one, 'privates', and infantrymen. Food was shared out generously to supplement the German ration of soup, and this was not only satisfying to the famished body but also to the curious mind. It consisted of tinned meat and biscuits which had come from England in prisoners' parcels; which parcels arrived (they were informed) with a regularly accountable only by a surprising honesty among people not universally famed for it.

'Well, that's one good mark we must give to Jerry!' exclaimed Willie, remembering the many opportunities there must be pilfering upon a long railway journey through enemy country.

'Divil a one at all,' was the reply of Paddy, 'only, regulations says they mustn't, and devil a one has the guts to disobey 'em, though they'd pinch the shirt off their own grandmothers!'

The laughter which followed this declaration was mixed with serious approval of its sentiments.

'Tis their deescipline only,' agreed Jock. 'When that breaks, we'll get no parcels through, but we shan't mind that – for why, we'll have won the warr. It's not honesty ye ken. 'Tis deescipline and a habit of it, that's the strongest in the worrld!'

This also received common assent.

'It's discipline,' said another, 'and yet 'tisn't discipline. It's fear.'

'I see what you mean,' said Willie. 'the same thing that keeps them honest, makes them murder women.'

'That's right, mate. I've known plenty o' decent Germans since I come here in September 1914. I've done 'em good turns, and they've done me some too but any of 'em would turn the kick for nothing, and kill me in cold blood, if he was told to. An Englishman keeps his blinkin' soul even when he is disciplined, but a German don't. And that's why them and me don't get on.'

Then with a grin of kindness the speaker turned to the lining of his great coat – 'You thank Mike, I ain't honest mate!' he said, and produced two eggs. 'Pinched 'em off the farm today, so they'll be all right,' he said, and handed one to each of the new comers, with a request to 'swaller 'em down!' Almost with tears they refused. The ready generosity of the act touched deep chords (as kindness must) and its humour brimmed the cup.

'Thank God, we're here with English – I mean British – pals!' exclaimed Willie. 'Amen,' quaintly concluded his companion: whereat all laughed.

'You chaps ain't reg'lars are you?' enquired one.

'No,' said Willie. Then came a fire of questions as to regiments now on the western front, casualties, movements, the general position, and the prospect (if any) of peace that year. These answered, Willie asked them questions. What was the work like?

'Easy.'

'What were the chances of escape?'

'Easy also, as far as getting away went. But you needed civilian clothes, and the lingo to help you. Holland was a long way off. It meant a week's travelling, or more. Harvest was past and that meant little concealment and little to live upon unless you carried your food. Three men had tried it and one was shot.

'Did the others manage it?' asked Willie.

'No, they got recaptured, and sent down the salt mines,' was the grim reply. 'You'd best let it alone, mates.'

'Humph!' grunted Willie. He had heard about those salt mines. The tales were not sweet to recall.

'I should think that the chap who got shot was the luckiest of those three,' he said.

'That's likely,' agreed the rest.

'Do – do they give you a medical examination?'

'Why, you ain't wounded, mate, are you?' said the man addressed, answering Private Gain.

'No. I just wondered, that's all. I was afraid ... I mean, I thought that when you came first you might have to 'pass through,' or something.'

'No, nothin' o' that. A doc' comes round if anybody's sick, and you get stuff pumped into yer arm or chest fer inoculation once now and then – that's all.'

'Oh!'

Willie wondered by what means his companion had evaded that fatal test on enlisting. It was but one of a series of questions his curiosity was determined to solve. Circumstances compelled him to put it aside with the rest.

'I'd like to write home,' he said. 'Is that allowed?'

'Yes. Letters are censored, of course. They take about three weeks to get to England,' was the answer.

'That's not bad.'

'No. You and your mate'll want some paper and ink. Here's some ...'

But just then a German soldier shouted 'lichts ans!' and passing down the hut, left its occupants to find their beds in darkness. Then someone noticed the little ghost of a new moon. One man went so far as to take a sovereign from the heel of his boot to turn it for good luck. Paddy blessed himself with the Cross. How typical, thought Willie, of the nation to which they belonged.

CHAPTER II

Next morning they were roused by a bugle-call, and after lining up with the rest of the prisoners, detailed for duty on a small farm about two miles off.

A German sentry escorted them to the place, gave them into charge of the farmer, and departed saying that he would call for them at the end of the day, and that they would be punished if the report of their day's work was not satisfactory.

Will had anticipated that he and his companion would be set to work together in the fields, but he was disappointed. The old farmer and himself went off to make a swede-pile. His comrade was kept to cart manure from the farm yard in company with the farmer's daughter – a fair muscular girl of about nineteen.

The four sons had been called away upon military service, and three were at the front. Already the work of the country was being done by women and old men, but this was the more natural because upon the continent women have never ceased to participate in labour of the fields.

Willie's curiosity must wait: his questions remain unanswered. He set himself whole-heartedly to appreciate the old man's design for the swede pile, finding it similar in most respects to that he had seen constructed by his father's workmen – Bill Trigg and the rest – in fields of home. Agriculture knows little of nationality.

Yet to have seen a thing done, is far different from doing it, and he must concentrate all his wits upon the work in order to avoid mistakes. He asked, and the farmer showed him by signs what was required, and since he was a willing worker, though not a skilled artist, he reached the end of the day with a good character. No one, at any rate, suspected that he was not what he pretended to be – a farm labourer.

In the meantime his fellow soldier had, though a stroke of fortune, made a good impression, which was later to stand them both in good stead. It happened that in leading the horse to stable after the cart-

175

ing was done an old hen that had been pecking about in the manger became startled at their entry and uprose with a great henish fluster into the animal's face, causing him to turn and knock down the German girl who was leading him in. Undoubtedly he would also have trampled over her in his attempted flight from the stable had not the English soldier struck him heavily on the nose with a fork-handle, and dragged the girl to one side, before the blow-arrested animal, persisting in his course, left the bewildered fowl in possession.

All this was related in excited German to the farmer upon his return, and he (having beaten the horse and cursed the hen) related it to the sentry. They marched back without opportunities of conversion that was not essentially casual, picking up other parties on the way.

That night Willie wrote home.

'Dearest, By the time you receive this you will have heard of poor Eric's death – or, possibly both of us will have been reported as 'missing'. But certitide is better than the suspense of that word. He was shot painlessly and suddenly on the morning of my capture. For me, do not worry! I am a prisoner, but well treated, and working on a farm in Westphalia. Parcels are permitted, and, as you see, letters. This camp holds about fifty prisoners – dear men of all sorts. We work in the fields by day and come back at night to sleep, so it is quite different from solitary confinement, or even prison life unbroken by activity that is craved by all men whether in or out of company. The same sun shines upon us both and the same stars. If Eric does not enjoy them (as I believe he does) it is because he has better things. He died as he lived, and as he wished to die, in a crusade; and has found the fruit of his steady growing. My heart is sad for you – there alone – but not for him, though at first I could not remember his sweet fruition, feeling only our loss and wishing to revenge him. Queer things have happened, of which I hope to tell you sometime in England. I do not understand them – yet. But of all that has befallen, nothing I feel now, is less tragical than Eric's end. So do not grieve for either of us, dearest. He is near you now, and I shall return – sometime. May it be soon! Ever your loving son. WILL.'

Mrs Harvey sitting quietly by the fire (as were at that hour almost every one of the mothers of England whose only sons had been posted 'missing') received this news in less dramatic circumstances than novelists have any right to impose upon their characters. Her circumstances, in common with those of the majority of farm owners during the war, had improved. Rents, which are based on profits, had risen. In her case, the farmers had offered to increase them. It must therefore be taken that the increase was no more than they could afford to pay. Her other investments being gone, she was naturally glad.

Yet how little luxury (which was not hers) or even comfort (which was) can direct happiness is plain when we consider that she sat there that evening no more or less disconsolate than thousands of other women who had lost their sons.

'Missing' was equivalent to 'lost'. Yet life is seldom so good or so bad as our dreams – even the outer husk of it! And that night she received Willie's letter.

It is fortunate for common people that life is not designed by even the best novelists. Take the present case:– Eric would have been kept to see the frustration of all his hopes in the treaty of Versailles. Willie would have returned home having been nursed to physical health and spiritual decay by Mrs. Bramsbury-Stuart:– kept alive for the purpose. This letter of his would have miscarried or reached Mrs. Harvey to be read in dramatic circumstances of financial disaster – the undertone to her son's adventures. In short, the story would be vastly improved by simultaneous tragedies trotting like black horses in tandem, with the guiding author astride.

Providence is very unkind to novelists. But He is kinder to them than they are to Him. As for common folks it is, as we have noted, fortunate that He, and not they, are life's designers. Reality may be less readable, but it is a lot more livable, and a lot more romantic to all but short-sighted people.

This is not a criticism, but an apology. It is an apology from life to art that it is unable to be so symmetrical in design! so perfect in tragedy.

It is an apology which will not be accepted by those myopic persons who put the tale above the Truth. But at the cost of remaining unread: acknowledging 'artistic' sins, yet persisting in them: this writer will abide in company with life as he has seen it: fearing more to be false to that, than to offend the great critics upon whom his bread depends.

More, he will say this, that though 'art as the criticism of life' is a maxim so famous that its converse seems to-day no other than heresay; yet first to last the converse is true. Life is finally the only criticism of art.

Which necessary digression having been set down to be read, or skipped, by the reader; we leave this old mother to her cry over Willie's letter, and return through space and time to Germany.

There came a day when Will and his gypsy companion found themselves working together in the fields and at bait hour stood together alone under the hedge wet with dew-drops which never dissolved that time of year in the wintry sun.

'Gypsy, you made my brother to go un-revenged, but you saved my life, and I want to ask pardon for hitting you so brutally,' said Willie.

'It was given long ago,' said she, standing a strange sight in her soldier's clothes; that is to anyone who knew her for a maiden.

'There are a lot of other things I want to ask,' said Will, 'but you need not answer them.'

'I will answer anything you ask me as well as I can,' was the reply.'

'How did yo get round the medical examination in England?'

'I took the place of another on the same night as he had passed through.'

'Whom?'

'A soldier I met. He joined the Warwicks a few days later, I believe.'

'Why did he consent to this'

'Because he didn't like his sergeant, and because I asked him. He wasn't a Gloucestershire man. I told him I was anxious to join his regiment but had been rejected by the doctors – I was in man's clothes.'

'Why so?'

Because I wanted to join up. I changed into his uniform and became Private Gain in the Gloucesters.

Willie laughed.

'Were you like the real Private Gain?'

'Not much, except that we were both dark, and about the same size; but they had only seen him a few times, and couldn't tell the difference.'

'How did you manage the changing business?'

'Behind a hedge, in the dark.'

'The Warwicks are in our division. Have you ever seen him since?'

'I think so, once, on a divisional field day.'

'Did he see you?'

'I don't know.'

'He wouldn't talk, would he?'

'I should think not. He'd get himself into trouble, you see.'

'Well, he's not likely to see you now anyway.'

'No.'

'Why did you wish to join the Gloucesters?' asked Willie.

'Because I wanted to.'

Willie roared. 'Well, there's no need to say anything about your sex, after all,' he chuckled.

'Something drove me to it,' she added.

'What?'

'I don't know.'

'Well, it's changed you, miraculously,' mused Willie.

'Has it? How?'

'I don't know. Perhaps it hasn't. Perhaps it is life that has changed. Then you were in a lovely setting, and suited it. Now – I can't think of you as the same girl, however, I try.'

'But, I am, I am!' Private Gain burst into tears.

'Yes, of course you are. There, don't cry,' pleaded the embarassed Willie.

The farmer was approaching with 'Prinz' and the cart. Prinz was a white ox embodying Germany at her best:– the tireless industry 'ohne hast ohne rast' which yet remained to her, though it had turned feverish; the good nature that had departed, and been replaced by blood-lust; the Mozart innocence and contentment of soul that had given way to bellowing and blare:– not that Mozart is like an ox, but that an ox may be like Mozart. And this ox was. He took you by his very look back to childhood and good fairies.

Viewing him you bethought all those gentle princes transformed by evil witches in the tales of Grimm. You recalled 'Beauty and the Beast':– at least Willie did, as his strange companion having brushed the tears aside with the sleeve of her tunic, stood for an instant or two fondling his brass-tipped horns, and curly poll.

The farmer himself (though he was not particularly kind to animals) regarded the beast with a reverence little less than that with which he regarded the Kaiser – and very much more affection.

Prinz was the only animal he ever spoke to – though he might shout at others. Others included his daughter, and these two soldiers.

Yet the bark of this old man was worse than his bite, and occasionally he kindled to a grim gaiety of reminiscence. Being sixty years of age he had seen Germany made. He had seen it grow like a monstrous mushroom or toadstool to poison all who ate of it. His pride

179

in the growth was mixed with fear, but he was no politician. His reminiscences were personal rather than general; and grimness was their dominant note. He found his gaiety in recalling such things.

How, for instance, he – a schoolboy then – had played truant to witness in a crowd the last public execution that had taken place in that part of Deutchland.

It took place in a forest. The condemned man was taken in a cart to the spot. It was a queer cart and acted both as vehicle and scaffold. there were ladders down each side. The man was dressed fittingly. He wore no coat nor collar (a collar would have been unsuitable to the occasion), but a white shirt with black bows down the front. He was drawn backwards, his face to the tail of the cart. Some priests stood round him praying all the time. Guarding the prisoner, soldiers marched on either side. There were an unusual number of drummers. (Their presence will be appreciated by all who have ever taken note of the brass band which accompanies quack dentists when they perform their 'painless extractions' in public. An agonised expression upon the face of the patient may be accounted for by nervous apprehension – besides fewer people see it than would notice a shriek. Also, a brass band attracts attention and invests the central figure with a certain pomp). This man had done to death a girl, and flung her body into the river. He was a married man.

At the appointed spot the cart stopped and became a scaffold. The crowd peered down from fir trees which they had climbed; or up, from the bare space nearer the prisoner, pressing upon the ring of soldiers. The prayers of the priests were drowned in a great drumming. Catching hold of the hair, grown conveniently long, someone 'stretched up his neck,' and the executioner severed it. All this the old farmer saw with his eyes from a tree. And he saw one other execution – the last in the whole of Germany. Then one of the condemned had danced upon the scaffold. She was 'an Austrian lady', and her fellow victim, the man who had assisted her to kill her husband. Having pushed him into a river, they had beaten him with driftwood till he drowned. The man's face was whiter than his white shirt with the black bows. There was snow of the ground, and his face was as white as that ...

The reason why such stories should be related in this book is that they show up more vividly than three or four pages of description, the character of the man whose pleasure was in relating them.

Yet, lest too sinister an expression seem to be given him thereby, it is necessary to remember how many beside neurotic sensation-seeking females throng 'The Old Bailey' to hear men condemned to death. The author himself was one time acquainted with an London bus-driver old-fashioned enough to scorn petrol, who spent all his leisure in such a way. He could tell you the salient features of every important murder for forty years back. And this man was British to the backbone. His repartee was worthy of the best (and slowest days) of London traffic. He was a good husband and a kind father.

This German – Willie's master – was a less lovable man, but he was no monster. Both, had they been less industrious, would have been readers of the best 'shockers.' Being illiterate they went to life, instead of to art, for their entertainment. No man who has enjoyed Stevenson or Wilkie Collins can claim a right to sneer at them. He takes his enjoyment differently – that is all. And he probably constitutes a deal less sheer brain work then they, since he finds his dome of pleasure complete, and the scaffolding (except for one essential piece) removed; but they build it stone by stone: timber by timber, in the mind, even as the authors were compelled to build their books.

As for the girl – the blue-eyed health-coloured daughter of this old man – she possessed in a feminine way the same power of turning life into story. The romance (pseudo romance perhaps) to which she youthfully devoted her soul was naturally different, less grim; more subjective. But like that of her father, it took as material the queer accidents of life and like his, it fitted into that larger pattern of romance which is woven of life's common incidents.

It began from a moment when the young English soldier had pulled her from under the hoofs of a horse. How it developed may be glimpsed in the lunch-hour conversation between Willie and his companion upon a later day.

'I have heard from my mother.'

She sighed, having no mother perhaps: then –

'That is a sweet thing!' she said.

'It is. Both sweet and bitter.'

'Bitter?'

'Aye – It was a sweet letter but it left a bitter taste. It was full of kind English thoughts and county gossip, and it has made me home-sick for something I had almost forgotten – forgotten as a reality.'

'What might that be?'

'England. Oh, when shall I see her – my dear green land? Kind mother, harbouring my other dear mother like a sweet soul of the land itself, when shall I see you?' he cried with tears.

'Courage, mate!'

'Courage, who says I have not got that in me? But what use is it? It is courage to walk out of these fields (I hate them though they are so like our own!) and be shot three hundred miles from home? What hope is there of getting away and back to my mates who fight and perish for my England! To die ineffectually like a dog, shot down by German bullets; or to go mad in a mine, are the alternatives – these, or remaining here.'

'Are you so unhappy, then?'

'Unhappy:– Is there more unhappiness in hell!'

Then, I think I can get you out of it,' she said.

'You! How?'

'Since you are not happy here with – with the Germans,' she went on, 'and find your spirit in England –'

'No, in France, now!'

'Ah, yes, in France: I will try,' she sobbed, 'to –'

'You said that before. What do you mean? How is such a thing possible?' he asked, never noticing her eyes.

'A strange thing has happened. A girl; the daughter of the farmer, Greta; ha! ha! ha! has been talking to me.' Private Gain overcame his hysterics. 'She want me to settle down here, after the war, and to – to marry her.'

'Good Lord! But how is that going to help us?'

'I don't know – quite. I must get her to like me more.'

'More?'

'Enough to let me go – as –'

'Aw what?'

'As a woman will when she truly loves.'

'That is rather cruel – Still –'

'Yes, it is rather cruel. Still, why should she not suffer as others must suffer when they love real men?'

The arrival of 'Prinz' the enchanted and his master cut short the conversation.

CHAPTER III

Now here is 'a situation' wasted. How during a month one woman made love to another woman; was encouraged fiercely and cunningly, and finally induced (with lies) to make preparations for a double escape in man's clothing to an enemy country in which both comfort and a return of passion awaited her – this, divested of the alluring studies of sex (dear to moderns) and psychology (the religion) must be told in one sentence, for the reason that we are not concerned with it; but with another matter; the escape, not of Greta, but of her false lover, and Willie.

Private Gain, having convinced the poor girl that his father was a large farmer in England, persuaded her to fly with him; minimising dangers and demanding only a map, a compass, two suits of civilian clothing, andhelp in forging a passport, as her contribution.

Meanwhile he learnt the language – or so much as a constant application could acquire.

Thus, early in 1917, there lay in a loft above 'Prinz's' stall all that was necessary for the successful escape into Holland of two prisoners of war – all, that is, except what was in the lap of the gods.

Covered with clean straw, two brown-paper parcels tied securely with string awaited the spring which would cause them to sprout like bulbs into a strange blossom of hats, coats, maps, compasses, tinned food, and rucksacks. Spring would clothe the trees again, and dry up the marshes. In the spring lovers might journey together, finding dry ways, and the concealment of new foliage – and so might escaping prisoners.

For different reasons, three people waited eagerly and anxiously for what should befall 'im wunderschonen Monat Mai.' The German girl had a pretty little song that began so. She taught it to Private Gain who whistled it on to Willie. He had heard that Schumann setting of Heine's poem before at a fashionable concert in England. It surprised him that it should be sung by an ignorant farm girl, and asked his companion to enquire what other songs Greta knew. Private Gain then proceeded to memorise half a dozen other tunes of similar type which included a delightful little 'Volksliedchen' (Schumann) and Schubert's gay and lovely 'Das Wandern.'

How had she learnt these? At school: from her mother: and from her father! Her two brothers – now at the front – knew many more songs than she. This information caused Willie to think again. How many lovely songs were known and sung even by cultured people in England? All his life long he had thirsted for music, and wasted his money attending popular concerts. Beyond a smattering of oratorio, a few symphonies, and one unforgettable performance of 'The Dream of Gerontius' gained at the Gloucester Festival, and the occasional snatched joys of visits to Queen's Hall – what did he know? Nothing. What did the ordinary man know? Less than nothing. He had never even heard the names of Purcell, Byrd, Morley, Willbye, Orlando Gibbons, – the composers of an age when England was musically supreme in Europe. He had not the faintest suspicion that England was once more being raised to that position by such men as Elgar, Stanford, Hubert Parry, Vaughan Williams, Bantock, Holst, Goossens, Howells, Bliss, and Ivor Gurney.

Willie, having once heard the famous cycle of Stanford's 'Sea Songs' sung at Gloucester: the singer being that quite inimitable artist, Plunket Greene: knew enough of what was going on, to guess at the rest: no more than that. The rich mine of English and Scottish folk-song, and incomparably the richest mine of any in Europe – the Irish – these were still undiscovered to him. And he was an enthusiast! What could the ordinary man know of them? Again – nothing. They were all shamed by one German peasant: a foolish sentimental girl, whose brain was no bigger than a bull-frog's.

Music and poetry – so that had been led to believe – were not for them: were not, like the English air, part of their heritage: their birthright!

'By God, it almost makes one wish that one were a bloody German!' was the exclamation which, though unuttered, shaped itself in Willie's mind as he thought of these things. That his own people, possessing a literature unexampled; a music only less worthy of praise than that of the land which produced Bach; a school of nature painters nowhere excelled:– that Englishmen should be fed with lies, and so led to despise its artists, and all the loveliness which had by them been left in trust for the generations, seemed a species of outrage: a treachery which murder hardly dwarfed.

This State-supervision of the Hun's: this kultur now inspired by militarian: has led to servility, and so on to murder under orders: but at least it is not guilty of neglecting its children, and shutting them out from comradeship with those spirits whose speech is of peace and joy.

'They are educated: we arn't and that,' said Willie, 'is all about it.' Then, very practically, he put the grievance from his mind, for there was nothing to be done. Problems of a pressing and personal kind became immediate. Thus one evening when a thin layer of crisp snow covered the ground they arrived back to find five new prisoners, and among them a slight Jewish-featured boy who eyes Willie's companion curiously as they entered the lighted hut.

'You are a Gloucester, mate, ain't you?' he asked.

Private Gain started. – 'Yes.'

'Expect you don't remember me –'

'No.'

'Nor changing clothes in a field –'

'Changing clothes – no!'

'Well, I'd a taken me oath – '

Willie stepped in with the offer of a tinned tongue – 'I dare say you are hungry, mate. Get outside this. It's from England, and better than the Jerrys will give you.'

That cut short the talk, and enabled his companion to escape for the time being.

'Well, of all bad fortune!' said Willie next day, talking to his mate in shelter of 'Prinz's' stall. 'Do you think he suspects the truth – that dark fellow?'

'He recognised me.'

'Yes, and now he knows that you told a lie in your denial, that doesn't matter. But does he suspect anything else?'

'That I am a girl? I don't think so. Why should he?Nobody else does.'

'It wouldn't matter much if anybody of the others did. They are all decent men. But there is something about this new chap that I don't like.'

'What?'

'I don't know – his eyes; I mistrust him.'

'But what could he do to us – what harm?'

'What may not a base man do? Even a fool might do us harm – any and every harm, with so much as we have now at risk. If the truth should get to German ears all our fine chance of escape is ruined.'

'Then had we best go soon?'

'Look at the snow falling. Think of the bare country .. . this border marshes! No, we will wait. But we must watch ... watch him carefully, and be prepared.'

That evening in the hut the new comer regaled the company with lewd stories. That is nothing. Every man tells lewd stories (exceptions being, it is said, Mr. Bernard Shaw and Oscar Wilde). But these were personal (he re-lived them) and not funny. On top of that they were told with a leer. It is the laugh that redeems such tales – as Chaucer knew well. Willie noticed that the leer was frequently in the direction of Private Gain.

'Stow it!' he cried at length. The Birmingham tyke measured him up and down, and decided to do so. Each knew then that he had made an enemy.

The situation fell from bad to worse without delay. Two days later Jenkins (that was his name) was caught stealing a fellow prisoner's food, and thrown into a pond for punishment. It was Private Gain who caught him. 'You'll be sorry for this,' cried the dripping thief, 'you bitch!'

Now that is a queer phrase to apply to a man ... Being neither of them fools both Willie and his companion knew then that it was now but a question of time before their secret would be published, not to the prisoners, but to the Germans.

'Whether he knows or not (and I think he does) his suspicions are enough to pique the Hun curiosity. They will find an excuse for a medical examination. Then we are ruined,' said Willie.

Red and white by turns, his companion assented.

'We must go,' she said, 'at once.'

But it happened at that time that they were engaged in sawing wood under cover and in company with the old farmer whose eye was always overlooking them. So for two days – snow still falling – and on the third Jenkins, that cur, was seen currying favour with the German feldwebel.

'Thank God he has got no parcels out yet!' thought Willie, who knew that the short and sure way to the German's favour was paved with tinned meat. 'Thank God, too, he knows no German; and the feldwebel but little English. Still,' he concluded, 'this can't go on.'

'Gypsy,' he said next day, 'you must make arrangements to go as soon as possible. Things are very unsafe ...'

That evening the feldwebel was presented by the enemy with a tin of stolen bully beef, and a conversation ensued which left the German laughing – a little incredulously. The English which the feldwebel knew was little but enough for the occasion. But as its result an order was received that Private Gain should report himself the following night for medical examination.

PART VII

ESCAPE

CHAPTER I

Snow married to rain produced an offspring that was both and neither. Sulky sleet (a snivelling unworthy baby of storm) dispirited the day with its peevish weariness. Snow in the air; rain upon the ground; it fell, melting instantly; and veiled with a cold misery all distances in earth or sky. Low ugly vapour took the place of clouds. There was no heaven. The earth was mud – just mud.

They squelched out – these two captives – to the farm thinking many things; saying nothing.

Prinz, the ox, awaited them already harnessed. Snow fell upon his snowy hide and was turned by the steady heat of his blood to water trickles. He looked like a snow-ox beginning to melt.

The old German was indoors – suffering from rheumatism. They stepped inside to take his 'orders for the day,' and exchanged a quick and joyous glance on being told that while the daughter attended to household duties (and her sire) they were expected to employ the morning carting hay to the outlying beasts, using the return journey to cart back firewood from the forest.

Willie led the ox round under the hay loft, where his confederate flung down fodder, one or two armfuls to deaden the fall of a heavier bundle; then more hay.

Willie had covered up this first escape kit and stood awaiting the fall of the second when Greta appeared. The girl had evidently been seen, from the loft, for as long as she stood chatting beneath, only fodder was thrown down.

Then, 'No more,' she cried out, and stood waiting for her soldier to descend. He came out of the stable having descended the inner ladder, and walked straight up to them. He was empty handed. As he came he buttoned his khaki overcoat more closely against the weather.

Then the old man called his daughter from the house ...

'Auf wiedersehn!'

They moved off. The girl looked back as she entered the house.

'Now back for the kit!' whispered Willie. His companion led on. 'Gypsy.'

'I've got it.'

'God it? When? Where?'

'I've got it on.'

The military overcoat was pulled open, and revealed civilian attire beneath.

'By Jove! That was good work' said Willie.

'Yes.'

They went steadily on, leaving the farm buildings behind them. Nothing could have been simpler; less exciting. Yet their two hearts were thumping hard.

'Everything's gone now except the wind and a bit of light – and God, I suppose He's up in the stars in bed.'

'I wish we were, Gypsy.'

They were whispering together in a forest where woodland whispers covered up theirs. They were alone – at last.

Night had fallen, but night was no time for rest. Rather its blanket dark, star-eaten concealment, and a command to trudge forward with all speed in the knowledge that at dawn it would be whisked away exposing them to a thousand perils.

Escaping prisoners must reverse the biblical phrase: 'Walk while it is yet night. For the day cometh when no man can walk – with safety.'

Guided by the north star glimpsed fitfully through forest boughs, they shambled on as fast as uneven ground and a tangle of undergrowth permitted; often stumbling; falling from time to time, but making progress: making for safety. Making for safety, but through danger, as we shall see. For escape is the least part of a prisoner's hardships. His troubles truly begin when he is 'out,' and every man's hand against him, and every dog's nose.

The wind and leaves in motion gave them a sense of being followed but in fact deadened the sound of their scuffling steps and made for safety. The clinging bushes which seemed so like human shapes served as an excellent camouflage to their own shapes. Soon they ceased to be frightened into panic: ceased to halt, trembling, gripping an arm. They proceeded at a good pace, keyed up for real danger but proof against the imaginary. The stars paled, wheeling westward before the coming of dawn. They had reached a clearance in the wood and just then a sudden light was flashed upon them like a policeman't bullseye. But it was only policeman Day. And he came not to detect but to warn, for the flash which had frighted them into rooted figures was reflected from a glass window. Where there are windows, there are men – presumably.

'Back into the undergrowth!' Like weasles they disappeared. Then, trembling, and checking the sound of their panting breath, they turned to watch. Only the hammer hammer of their two hearts ... They thanked God that no cock crew to be answered by others, that no dog barked, that no smoke waved into plume blue against gold. The house, cottage, or whatever it might be, was isolated. Possibly it was a Woodman's hut. But was it inhabited? And did it contain food? And had it a spring of water? They lay listening for a time and watching intently. Then a whisper, 'Don't move!' Willie, escaped prisoner of war, had turned into Willie, a scout of the Gloucestershire Regiment. He disencumbered himself of impediments, and slid away upon his belly. His companion lay obediently still, in covering shade, watching with bright brown fairies eyes the crawl, the crouch, the little run from bush to bush, and the final wriggle beneath that blazing star – the window.

Willie rose to his feet and gave one quick glance into the hut. She expected to see hi bob down again immediately – in the same movement. He remained standing. He turned and waved her towards him. She cleared the open space at a run and was at once standing beside him.

'Is it empty?'

'No.'

'No! What – ?'

'Look in!'

Screwing her eyes into pin points, she put her face against the warm glass. She did not notice the touch of it then. What she saw took away all other sensations. A man outstretched upon the floor. He lay motionless upon his back. Flies were on his face.

'Dead?'

'Dead, or dead drunk.'

'Oh!'

'Will find out.'

She took that as an invitation to follow him round the ramshackle hut to find the door. Would it be locked? It was not. It opened with a loud creak. Back both jumped round opposite corners. Still the man never stirred. They tiptoed in. Willie crept forward and hurled himself upon the figure, grasping it by its throat. It was it – not him. The head wagged horribly to and fro as Willie shook it. It was dead. And it smelt dead. Willie got up looking very pale. Behind him stood Gypsy with a knife in her hand.

'What are you doing with that?'

'I was afraid of what he might do to you.'

'Well, put it away now, my dear. There's no need for it. And remember, you must not commit murder even for me. They hand you for it.'

'If you were dead I should want them to hang me – but they wouldn't do it.'

'And why not?'

'Because I should kill myself.'

Willie looked at her curiously. From chalky-white her face gradually glowed to a golden-brown, the gypsy was blushing. Then she swayed forward into his arms and lay there sobbing. Willie soothed her, kissing her forehead.

The dead man regarded by cynically. He had done with all such human folly.

'Come, this won't do! You search the place, I'll search his pockets. There may be something useful to us – a passport.'

There was no passport. But the cavernous cupboard revealed some mouldy black bread and a little round cheese. Willie cut the cheese into slices, pocketing what they could not then eat. Water from a spring which bubbled up almost in the hut's doorway served to wash down the meal which they took out into the wood.

Before leaving, Willie crammed the corpse into the cupboard. It very nearly fitted, but not quite. The buzzing flies would help hide it anyway. He locked the door with the key which they had found, and dropped it into the spring. It would not do to be caught with it. Perhaps the man had been murdered. Whether or no, someone would almost certainly come to look for him. That is unless he were an escaped prisoner like themselves, and the hut no longer in use.

Whatsoever he might have been, he was dead, and they were alive. That was a point – alive … and lovers.

Recumbent in undergrowth they munched, and talked in whispers. A few hundred yards away their dead host occupied his own cupboard.

CHAPTER II

The weather had improved beyond recognition. The moisture upon the leaves evaporated. A few diamond drops flashed downwards from pine-needles. The clothes of the escaping prisoners dried upon them as they rested, sleeping a little in turns but alert like dogs even in slumber – one ear cocked for danger.

It had been well said that some of the most significant encounters in the world occur between two persons, one of whom is asleep or dead. Willie lay watching over Gypsy who lay in slumber more deeply than usual.

O Sleep and Death, great magicians in a world of care, how can you make attractive the face the least attractive, and bestow dignity upon the least dignified! Chiselled as if in marble the face of the gypsy girl conquered the shade in which she lay. Her form sun-dappled and flecked with shifting shadow fought through its moulding garments of rough cloth as her soul seemed to shine through its covering of mortality, quiet and unabashed in innocent nakedness. It was awesome, almost frightening. Willie toughed her chin lightly. Instantly she sat upright, alert. As a stone shatters the deep heaven reflected in a lake, so broke to bits the lovely vision shattered into particles of care, anxiety and fear. She was awake.

'What is it?'

'Nothing. Somehow I couldn't watch you asleep any longer. Forgive me!'

'Oh, are you lonely?'

'Well, in a way. You seemed to have gone so far away.'

'But I was dreaming of you. Now you seem to have gone so far away from me.'

'Yes, both of us are awake.'

'What time is it – I mean, is it time to go on?'

No, too light. We'll talk till the sun is hidden.' They did so in whispers. That is – their hearts asked and answered inconsequent questions, while their senses kept watch for danger always with pricked ears.

Gypsy: When did you see me first?

Willie: I have never seen you. In the Forest of Dean I first met you.

Gypsy: No. It was a year before that.

Willie: Where?

Gypsy: At Barton Fair. In the shady market at Gloucester.

Willie: Then I never saw your face.

Gypsy: You did not, but your eyes were boring holes through my back. I felt them.

Willie: Were you she then in the shawl? I might have known it. I went home and wrote your description.

Gypsy: Back view! Was it nice?

Willie: My essay was. I showed it to Mother.

Gypsy: What did she say?

Willie: Oh, she admired it.

Gypsy: But what did she say of me?

Willie: Shall I tell you?

Gypsy: Yes.

Willie: She said – 'You have imagined her.' I said, 'Men only imagine women, even when they are married to them.' She smiled. 'But would you like to marry her' she asked. 'I don't know,' I muttered. then Mother said, 'You could not love her indoors, nor she you.' Are you sorry now that you asked?

Gypsy: No. She was a wise Lady … But can you remember any of what you wrote about me?

Willie: Bits here and there. But the rhythm of the prose which was beautiful as your walk under the market trees – that has gone from me … Only sentences here and there come back as I look at you.

Gypsy: Go on.

Willie: 'She shone like a queen through her rags.'

Gypsy: (indignantly) I was not in rags!

Willie: It was because you were so fair in yourself that they looked 'rags' upon you.

Gypsy: Seemed I so, then, to you, dear love?

Willie: Among the fine ladies and gentlemen you walked with your basket. The ladies looked common beside you; like pictures on a chocolate box, and they would have tasted like chocolate creams. 'But she was like no other girl I ever saw. Elevated like a wave, or the wind on a meadow. All nature closed round her like a frame. Nakedness which would have shamed those others would but have glorified her. Petty lust could not touch her, but only wonder – and worship.'

Gypsy: And was that how you felt? Oh, poor boy!

Willie: And so it ended – To desire her would be to desire a big thing, not a pettiness. To that bosom one would leap as one leaps into the salt sea for vigour and cleansing. In her beauty was something of terror as in all things elemental.

Gypsy: Aye, outdoor likenesses all. You would not say to her, 'come, dust my room,' nor ask for your slippers. O Lady Mother was right! My grief!

Willie: Lady Mother! My grief! But you talk like an Irish woman.

Gypsy: I picked it up, I suppose, going over there with my Dad to buy nag-horses.

Willie: You have moved about a lot.

Gypsy: I never knew a fixed home and never shall.

Willie: We shall see about that.

Gypsy: Hush, listen.

A faint drone drifted upon the air, increased in volume beating tattoo upon their ear-drums. A black speck appeared upon the fading gold of the west. An aeroplane.

'Can it be searching for us?'

'Perhaps, or perhaps for other escaped prisoners. It can't land here anyway. Keep perfectly still, and at dusk we'll be off.

The aeroplane droned slowly over them. Its engine roar diminished. From a white gigantic bird of fury shining in the last high rays of the sun, it dwindled to a black speck floating upon the evening air, and at length vanished.

The lovers shouldered their impediments and began another march. But first they filled their water bottles from the dead man's spring.

CHAPTER III

Marching by night, led by the noble north star; resting by day, sleeping a little, but alert even in sleep: whispering a little: so, progressing painfully and slowly through innumerable dangers they kept their slow but steadfast way, approaching ever nearer the frontiers of Holland – of Hope. They were lovers. It was in once sense a perilous honeymoon. Yet they talked little of love. By the fourth day their blood was very thin. They were very cold, always in hunger and athirst – especially athirst. They huddled together for comfort as they lay exhausted in a ditch and timorously hidden under bare leafed bushes or amid the brown haired reeds which sighed and swayed, shivering above them as in sorrow of their plight.

Only their hearts glowed. Only their hearts were strong. For the rest, every nerve and sinew was now utterly exhausted.

'I can go no further.' Gypsy spoke or rather gasped the admission of her body's defeat.

Willie had already taken her bundle, and the double weight, small as it would have been to a young soldier on the march, caused his knees to sag, and made every step a stumbling agony of effort.

He, as well as his comrade, was spent.

'We will take the road thus. Lean a little on me but don't sit down. We will rest a bit standing. Lean here!'

She did as she was told.

They were in marshy country. It was hard on midnight. Since dusk they had trudged slowly, wearily – skirting roads and villages that taunted their homelessness with mocking window-lights that peered and leered from under dark eyebrows and seemed to cry, 'Why are you footsore and famished? Why do you not come to see us? Here is fire, light and food. Here is rest and shelter for all weary travellers – except of course escaping prisoners of war. Are you of those accursed outcasts?'

And oh, it had been such a struggle to resist those twinkling lights! But till now they had resisted.

'Yes, we must take the road,' gasped the girl, 'the lights are all dauted,' she added.

Munched field roots (stolen from swede piles), hard berries, raw seed potatoes: the dirty water scooped up from ditches and bog holes, had afflicted their bowels. Their strength was at snapping point. 'We will risk it,' he muttered. Together they staggered across the soggy waste and so up a bank to firm surfaces – the road.

'Go softly. This is dangerous. We must be very near the frontier' – he whispered her. So, forward they went.

It was, as the Germans say, 'as dark as a wolf's mouth.' They thanked God that it was. Yet every moment they feared the click of the wolf's teeth. At last it came – the click of a rifle both drawn and set back! A challenge! The flash of a lantern revealing a sentry box standing in the middle of the road!

Willie dropped everything and dived headlong down the embankment. As Gypsy followed, a bulled screamed past. Now they were on their feet and running as only terror could make them. But they kept together, more shots were fired. The sentry had summoned the guard. The lanterns they carried revealed only themselves to the pursued who ran gasping from them till suddenly both – falling – lay stunned. The bang made them believe they had been shot. He fumbled about in darkness. Gypsy lay motionless beside him. Killed? She did not reply to his frantic whisper. He crawled a yard upon hands and knees to seek water for her. If he had had a match at that moment he would have lighted it regardless of revealing himself, so frantic was his anxiety for her. His hand struck something cold. At that moment she gave a little moan. 'Where are we?' she asked faintly.

'Oh, thank God! thank God!' was all Willie could answer. 'Are you hurt?'

'No, but you must leave me. I cannot get up. Leave me!'

'Never!'

Willie's hand became conscious of the cold metal which it was grasping. He told his brain that they were lying in the middle of a railway track.

'Where are we?' moaned the girl.

'Wait, I will tell you. We are on a railway line. We are not wounded. Tell me,' he went on, talking with the most intense excitement. 'Tell me, Gypsy, are these sleepers wood or iron?'

'Oh, wood, I think. Yes, wood!'

'Yes, they are wood!'; shouted Willie at the top of his voice.

'Hush! are you mad, to shout so! they will find us, and I can go no further.'

'You need not go any further. And I can shout as loud as I like. We have crossed the frontier! We are in Holland!

In Holland? How do you know that?

'By the wooden sleepers, silly. Don't you know that the Germans use iron for sleepers, and the Dutch wood!

* * *

Willie, tattered, filthy, with five days growth of black chin-stubble (one could not dignify that facial fungus with the noble name of beard) sought out the nearest British Consul and reported himself. That pleasant, dignified personage was not at all shocked by his appearance. He was used to such apparitions. Escaped prisoners of war seldom arrived spotlessly clean. What knocked him right off his official manner was Willie's story of the escape. 'But do you – do you –,' he stammered, 'really wish me to believe that your companion was – was a woman!'

'A girl, sir. We escaped to side-step a medical examination. But I don't suppose she would object to it here in Holland. I should think she has had enough soldiering by now.'

'Good God! Good God! This is most – most –'

'It seems, if you will pardon me, sir, quite simple. She is examined by a doctor who certifies her of feminine sex. As a female, she cannot rejoin the fighting forces. She gets her discharge. All that remains, sir, is for you to issue her a passport to England.' (And it was so.)

* * *

Willie, upon reporting to his Home Depot, was granted a month's leave. Before that leave was up, the war had ended, and not till then did he again see his escaping comrade and sweetheart. For during that time his mother died.

CHAPTER THE LAST

Gypsy and Willie sat together at the edge of the coppice overlooking almost all of Gloucestershire and Herefordshire. It was a clump of trees upon the top of May Hill from which they had emerged.

Upon that purple, tree tufted bubble of earth, so lovely against the saffron sunset, these weeping children argued out their destiny.

'No, my love, I have given you myself – all I had to give.

'But now you are taking yourself away. Oh, you can't! You could not be so cruel! Marry me!'

'That would not be wise. Your Lady Mother knew it.' Her straight brown eyes looked into his with dog-like loyalty and affection, but her mouth was set in a woman's resolution. In the line of those red lips lay carved inflexibly her design.

'You will be a great man,' she said. 'Your world will not be the gypsies world, nor will the gypsies world be yours. Oh, I wish to God above it could be, my dear.'

'But,' he cried out in agony, 'have you no pity for me, for yourself, for either of us? The brother I loved is dead, and the mother I worshipped; you only, my sweetheart, are left to me in a world of wreckage and horrible loneliness!'

'I, too, shall be lonely.'

'Then why in the name of God of Love! –'

'No, my beloved.'

'But why?'

'You don't understand us. You call us gypsies. I won't correct you. You have made the name sweet to me. And all the rest of the world outside call us gypsies: and scorn us: yes, as we scorn them.

'Do you scorn me, Gypsy!'

'No, beloved.'

'Neither do I scorn you or yours.'

'Truly. But you will never understand us.'

'Must a man understand what he loves?'

'I suppose he needn't; nor a girl either. But you have talked me off the track. I will not marry you, my love. It would not be wise. Did not your –'

'Oh, for Christ's sake stop talking about my mother! She loved me. Yes, she loved me, but you –' sobs drowned his voice.

'I love you, too – for ever.'

'Yet you would part yourself from me!'

'Yes. Parting isn't for ever.'

The phrase came like an echo from another world. When had he heard it uttered before? Had he heard it before. Almost his Mother's voice seemed to speak it, or was it the voice of his brother, Eric. Why should the departed tones of his mother and his brother utter themselves through the red loving lips of a gypsy girl! And still he heard her speaking. 'I shall part from my lover. He will not know where to find me. But I shall be in his heart and he in mine. Yes, if you don't know where I am, my love, I shall always know where to find you.'

Again was it Gypsy, Eric, his Mother, or all three that were speaking.

She arose, and without looking back walked down the hillside into Herefordshire. His county lay to the further side of the hill. He tried to follow her, but found himself physically unable to call, but tears choked back his cry. Even so, with no embrace nor kiss, they parted. How utterly inartistic is sorrow!

Willie just sobbed. At first the sobbing was quite inarticulate. Gradually it became able to utter the formula of all grief in all ages from the cradle to the grave – a cry of anguish and a prayer in one. Oh, oh, oh, oh God! and again and again like the monotonous lines of some mad poet. Oh, oh, oh, oh, God! O God! If his heart was not breaking it was being re-born. As the horrible sobbing faded into little choking sounds, and finally died, a sentence sang like little far off bells in his brain or was it far off singing over and over again something he seemed to have forgotten and now remembered. Something somebody told him long, long ago and asked him to remember. Who was it? His Mother? Eric? Gypsy? Reverberating like distant bells – softly in his brain – 'If you don't now where I am, I shall always know where to find you, always! always! always! And like plangent peals over and over again –

'Parting is not for ever.'

He only heard them. He only went on hearing them. He did not understand them. He only heard them – these words, ringing, ringing – like bells in his brain. He only went on hearing them.

THE END

If you enjoyed this book, you may also be interested in…

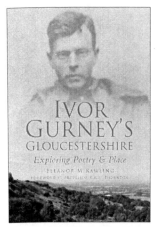

Ivor Gurney's Gloucestershire: Exploring Poetry and Place

ELEANOR M RAWLING

Ivor Gurney is perhaps best known as a musician and First World War poet but he also wrote vividly and prolifically about his native Gloucestershire, finding inspiration and joy in walking the countryside and expressing its different moods. This book contains a wealth of Gurney's poetry with many pieces being published here for the first time. There are four walking routes, with accompanying commentaries and poetry extracts. The author is a geographer, literary researcher and walker. Having been born and brought up in Gloucestershire, she has a passion for its landscapes and places.

978 0 7524 5353 8

Great War Britain

LUCINDA GOSLING

The declaration of war in August 1914 was to change Britain and British society irrevocably. Popular weekly magazines such as *The Tatler*, *The Sketch* and *The Queen*, recorded the national preoccupations of the time and in particular, the upper-class experience of war. Targeted at a well-heeled, largely female audience, these magazines were veteran reporters of aristocratic balls, the latest Parisian fashions and society engagements, but quickly adapted to war-like conditions without ever quite losing their gossipy essence. The result is a fascinating, at times amusing and uniquely feminine perspective of life on the home front during the First World War.

978 0 7524 9188 2

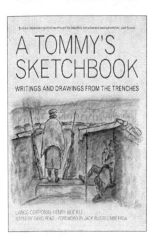

A Tommy's Sketchbook

HENRY BUCKLE

'Shall have to be about all night, for have charge of this particular bit of trench. Have now made close acquaintance with the brilliant lights we have seen breaking over No Mans Land. They are fired from a large pistol, one of which I have in my pocket now, also a supply of cartridges for same. ' Lance Corporal Henry Buckle's drawings and writings are a window onto the Western Front as one man saw it. His charming colour sketches are a rare and exquisite insight into trench life that cannot fail to amuse and move the observer. This book truly allows you to experience the Great War at first hand..

978 0 7524 6605 7

Visit our website and discover thousands of other History Press books.

www.thehistorypress.co.uk

Lightning Source UK Ltd.
Milton Keynes UK
UKOW04f2153100614

233171UK00001B/12/P

9 780750 959711